SICK PIGEON

SICK PIGEON

M.A.C. FARRANT

THISTLEDOWN PRESS LTD.

© M.A.C. Farrant, 1991
All Rights Reserved.

Canadian Cataloguing in Publication Data

Farrant, M.A.C., (Marion Alice Coburn) 1947-

  Sick pigeon

  ISBN 0-920633-83-8

I. Title.

PS8561.A773S5 1991   C813/.54   C91-097108-0
PR9199.3.F377S5 1991

Book design by A.M. Forrie
Cover illustration by Gisèle Beaupré
Author photo by Terry Farrant
Typeset by Thistledown Press Ltd.

Printed and bound in Canada by
Kromar Printing Ltd.
725 Portage Ave.
Winnipeg, MB R3G 0M8

Thistledown Press Ltd.
668 East Place
Saskatoon, Saskatchewan
S7J 2Z5

This book has been published with the assistance of The Canada Council and the Saskatchewan Arts Board.

Acknowledgements

The author thanks the editors of the following magazines where these stories previously appeared: *NeWest Review, Waves, Going Down Swinging* (Australia), *Fireweed, Writ 20, Secrets from the Orange Couch, Random Thought.*

Thanks also to Norman Wright and Joan Henriksen for their generous loan of Scow House.

For Terry

CONTENTS

Sick Pigeon 11

Stealing George 20

Rob's Guns and Ammo 30

The Loneliest Sound You'll Ever Hear 39

Side by Side 44

The Bible in Longhand 53

Call Out of Nowhere 65

All the Good and Beautiful Forces 70

Macaroni and Cheese 82

Club Sandwich 87

French Fries 92

SICK PIGEON

So I found this pigeon, eh? Lying beside the sandbox in the park. Whimpering. Trying to flap its wings. Looked like it'd been hit with a rock or maybe a dog got it. And all kinds of people around too. Everyone walking around it like it was a turd or something. Didn't want nothing to do with it. I couldn't figure it out. I mean there should a been a crowd around that bird all deciding what to do. I mean there's this poor sick pigeon in front of them probably going to die and nobody's doing a thing. What's happening is a big fat zero. What's happening is worse than nothing. I mean what's happening is a crime. The way nobody cares. Just like them mice in cages and them poor, harmless bunnies. Doing experiments on them like some weird horror movie. The way nobody cares about them either. Killing for no good reason.

So yeah, yeah Sybilla, it's a rotten world. Full to overflowing with crazies. So what's new?

But Jesus, I'm thinking, leaving a bird like that to die. In broad daylight. I mean people. They make me sick.

I started to cry when Christian first showed me it. Then he starts to cry so now there's two of us crouched over that bird bawling our eyes out. Mommy, is it going to die? he says and I says, no way ho-zay, not if I can help it. That kid has a heart like mine, can't stand to see a thing suffer.

So we brought it home, eh? Then all those jerks in the park started staring at us. Where before we could a been dirt. I'm wrapping the pigeon in a baby's blanket and I'm putting it on the baby's lap in the stroller and everyone's giving us these disgusted looks like we was packing home a live rat or something. Moving away from us like we had the plague. Looking down on us. As usual. That's nothing new. Everyone's always looking down on us. Excepting maybe that worker Tony from when I was thirteen at the Treatment Centre. He never thumbed his nose at me, but then after a while he went away, never did hear from him again.

So what Sybilla? Tell us another one. You got some idea that shit and heartache ain't the price of admission?

Enough already, I says to myself, and pushes that bird out of the park, dragging Christian behind me. So there I am, eh? Slaving away with this buggy and not one of its wheels working right. And trying to shush the baby, she's got some bright idea that limp pigeon on her lap is a toy for playing with and all the way home she's banging at it with her bottle of Kool-Aid and screaming at me when I tell her to stop. End result is red Kool-Aid all over everything, ass to tea kettle, the baby, the pigeon, the blanket.

Then the sun starts to come out so suddenly it's a heat wave and we're three blocks from home and me, I'm sweating buckets and cursing myself, why'd I have to go leather today? Why couldn't I a gone shorts and thongs like all them other mothers in the park, those ritzy bitches who wouldn't give me the time of day even if I went begging for it.

You're up the creek without a paddle, Sybilla. Like always. You ain't running on a full tank.

So now I'm thinking, I hope this pigeon is grateful, what we're going through to save its life. It can thank its stars the day Sybilla found it and brought it home. And made it live. I make everything I find live. One way or another. Usually.

Live, you sucker. That's what I tell them, all the poor sick things. Take Gimp, for instance. Found her by the side of the road. Left for dead.

Ain't they all, you idiot. Ain't they all left for dead sometime? What about your own mother? Left for dead in a motel room. Drunk again. Choking on her own vomit.

Be quiet, I says to myself. I'll get to that. Right now it's animals I'm talking of. I'm talking of Gimp and how she'd been run over, her back all mangled. Can you picture what it's like to be run over?

S'cuse me while I throw up.

Yet there's cats all over the world regularly dragging themselves out from under cars, panting and gasping for air, looking for some kind person to save them. Lucky for Gimp she got me and not some creep who'd kick her into a ditch, not caring one small bit about her, probably even getting a thrill out of watching her die. Lucky old Gimp. Took nearly all my welfare cheque for the vet bills and we had to eat canned soup for a week but I pulled her through. So now she can drag herself around pretty good. Even had three litters which explains all the cats I got around my place right now. Seventeen of them. Not including Gimp. Plus a couple of strays. I got a way with animals. They gravitate to me like shit to a blanket. They know I'll look after them, one way or another. They all know Sybilla's here when they need her.

But anywho, back to the pigeon. Time we get home this pigeon's not looking too good, got red Kool-Aid all over his body and breathing funny. I was getting real worried. I don't like to lose them. So we gave it a bath, eh? Figuring that might help. And Christian who's a gentle kid for being only three years old held it in a towel and patted it dry. The baby I threw in the tub.

We was just getting ready to find a bed for the bird, somewheres the cats couldn't get at it, and maybe try to give it some water when I looks out the kitchen window and catch sight of Miss Hope, the Public Health Nurse, hustling her buns up the front path. Come for a visit, eh? Oh shit, I'm thinking, here comes trouble. So I says to Christian, quick Christian, take this bird and hide it somewheres in the bedroom away from the cats, we don't want Miss Hope finding it and causing a stink. She sees a sick pigeon in the house she won't shut up till Christmas. Next thing Miss Hope's rat-a-tatting on the kitchen door.

Are you crazy, Sybilla? Have you lost your marbles? There's garbage everywheres. Miss Hope takes one look in here she'll be yapping about disease and germs like always.

Jesus, I'm thinking, looking around the kitchen, what a holy mess. But that's the piss-off. These Miss Hopes and their like and every social worker I ever had the bad luck to know, they all figure when you're on Welfare they can drop in on you any old time. They're like those surprise bombers in the TV war movies. Come out of nowhere. Can't wait to drop their bombs on you.

Bang, bang, you're dead, Sybilla.

No letting a person know. And they really got it in for single mothers. At least I could a gotten rid of the cat dishes, maybe cleaned off the counter, made the place look decent. But no such luck. It's like they want to catch you with your pants down, always checking up on you to see if you're beating your kids yet. That's the one thing they live for, grabbing your kids. Like what happened to me. Grabbed from my mother when I was only eight years old. Just because she drank. They got no respect, all these do-good workers.

I get about as much respect from them as a flea would get. Maybe less. How about that? Maybe they figure Sybilla's not even as good as a goddamned flea.

Stop it. You're breaking my heart!

So rat-a-tat goes this Miss Hope on the door, eh? And I'm stalling and calling, just a minute lady, and grabbing the baby outa the tub and making sure Christian's hid the bird good enough and find he's stashed it under the pillows on the bedroom floor.

Then again this Miss Hope's rapping on my door, only this time it's louder and she's hollering, Sybilla open the door please, I know you're in there.

Of course I'm in here, you dumb broad, I'm thinking, you figure this is a bank robbery, you're the cops got the place surrounded? You figure I'm holed up inside? Like when I was at the Treatment Centre, the way I used to barricade myself in the girl's dorm. All those workers making me do stuff like I was a slave or something. Wash the floors. Clean the toilets.

So I just get enough time to grab the bird and shove it under the kitchen sink and while I'm racing with it I'm noticing it's stopped breathing and I'm thinking, oh shit, I think it's dead. And this is really upsetting me, this is really twisting my socks. I mean I hardly get a chance to work on it and already it's croaking?

And this damned banging on the door, it ain't quitting. So then I finally open the door, got the baby hanging off my hip, still wearing my leathers, never did get time to change. And what does this Miss Hope lay on me but, I've come about your animals, Sybilla, we've been getting complaints again.

So there's this Miss Hope standing on my front porch, eh? Wearing this pink pantsuit, looking very shit hot, got about a ton of make-up covering her wrinkles and red blush on her face about as red as a Valentine card. And moaning at me about having complaints again. And I'm going, Jesus, which one of these assholes around here finked on me this time?

I told them down at Welfare last year when they first got this dump, I told them then: I shouldn't be living in this prissy neighbourhood, you should have gotten me a joint in that new housing project where all the poor people live. Not shoving me in with all these high-class snots, always breathing down my neck, telling me how to live. I should be where all the real people are, in the housing project. They understand about saving sick animals and all the real problems of life.

But oh no, the Social Worker strung me some line about how this shitbox was all that was available and I was lucky I didn't have to live in some sleaze-bag motel. Yeah, great, I go, the only shitbox for miles around, stuck in the middle of a class act subdivision and I got to get it. A left-over shitbox at that. What they call an eye-sore. Walls like paper, the roof leaking and none of the locks on the doors work right. Last winter it was so cold and wet in here black mould started growing on the walls.

Poor old Sybilla. They figure that's all you're good for.

So I says to this Miss Hope, like who for instance ratted on me this time? I know for a fact who did it last time, that bitch down the road got shit for brains. Can't even control her own kids, always giving me the finger every time I go by. Talk about emotionally disturbed. And they said I was emotionally disturbed! Eight years old and thrown in a treatment centre for five years. Who wouldn't be disturbed?

Anywho, this Miss Hope says she can't tell me who complained, it's confidential information. *Confidential information!* She says she's just come to tell me the SPCA inspectors are coming around any minute now to make an investigation, there's been complaints, she says, of a large number of dead or dying cats lying in my front yard. She says. She says. Gimme a break.

So I slam the door in her face, eh? Get out of here you douche-bag, I'm screaming, my cats are all in beautiful shape, you got the wrong house, the only thing that's not in great shape in here is me and that's because bitches like you won't get off my back.

That fixed her. She took off then, got into her car slamming the door and drove off.

You tell her Sybilla. What does she know? Thinks she's so great in her pink pantsuit. You tell her where to get off. You tell them all where to get off.

I will, I'm thinking, pissed right out of my tree. I mean, no one's telling me how to live.

So what happens next, eh? but the baby starts howling and pretty soon there's Christian hanging off my leg and starting to cry. And that's all I'm needing. I start bawling too. Me and Christian and the baby, we're sitting on the kitchen floor, leaning against the cupboards and we're bawling our eyes out. It just ain't fair. Why can't they leave us alone? Just because I'm a single mother. Just because I'm only nineteen. Just because my kids got different fathers, I don't even want to think about those jerks. Just because I've got a kind heart.

Poor Sybilla. Got an "m" on your forehead the size of a billboard light. Poor, poor girl.

And then the cats start coming round us, there on the floor, frantic like, some of them purring, some of them hissing at each other. I know they're hungry, they finished the last bag of crunchies a couple of days back and my cheque's not due till Thursday. But I never have enough money, it all goes on these animals. Someone's got to look after them. All the SPCA does is kill them, right? Someone's got to care.

SICK PIGEON

So then I'm remembering about the pigeon, eh? And I'm feeling real bad thinking it's dead. I take it out from under the sink and have a look at it. Got to keep pushing the cats away, they're thinking it's something to eat. But the bird is so pretty, kind of a silvery grey colour with blue flecks in it. The sun's shining on it through the window and it's almost sparkling, like it was covered with tiny blue lights. So I start patting it and stroking its back. This makes Christian and the baby get real quiet and stop their bawling. So there we are on the kitchen floor, all looking down at this bird on my lap. The cats cruising around, still trying to get at the poor harmless thing. And I'm thinking, we'll have to bury it, have a little ceremony. Christian likes having a ceremony. He always puts one of his toys in the grave, a Hot Wheels car or something he's made out of Lego. So then I start thinking how everything's so sad. I mean, there's my poor dead Mom, never did get to see her again after they took me away. There's those guys who knocked me up then buggered off. You know, I'm thinking on all the miserable junk that passes for some kind of life when all of a sudden the pigeon gives a shudder and starts flapping its wings, trying to stand up. And now I'm so happy, I'm going, it's a miracle. This pigeon is alive after all, he's going to live. And I say to Christian, Christian we got to get him some water, it looks like this pigeon is going to make it. Maybe it had passed out or something before, maybe it was only sleeping.

So then I get the pigeon a drink, eh? I fill up the baby's bottle with water figuring to put the nipple into the bird's mouth the way I do with the sick cats, give them their water that way. And I'm feeling so great. I'm saving another life, this pigeon's going to live. And I'm feeling so great, eh? that I only get mildly twisted when I see the cop car pull up in front of the house, got its lights flashing red and blue. Then the SPCA van. Then Miss Hopeless in her dinky blue car. All of them crowding in front of my house.

And I'm thinking, it looks like I'll just be getting enough time to push the kitchen table against the door before they all come storming up the path. So I go to Christian, quick Christian, help me shove this table against the door, we don't want anyone bursting in and bothering us when we got important work to do. There's a sick pigeon here needing water and what do all these assholes know about that!

STEALING GEORGE

Cindy's my friend got worse troubles than me. She finally gets this baby George but something goes wrong. He's up at the hospital and Cindy feels so bad she calls me up. "Long time no see," she says. She wants to talk, mother to mother. Cindy's twenty-one been trying to get a baby since she was fourteen at Alderwood Treatment Centre so I know she's happy at having George. Only something's not right, she says. George's not breathing too good. And then she starts to bawl right over the phone.

Some people think it's funny for Cindy and me to be friends. She's this short, fat Indian and me, I'm this skinny white chick got dyed yellow hair. But I say, fuck'em all in the tits. Cindy and me, we once shared the girl's dorm at Alderwood and that makes us friends for life. She was in for B & E's. Me, for having a drunken Mom. They said I was acting unruly.

So Cindy comes for a visit, eh? and she's not looking too hot. Fact is, she looks like shit. Looks like she's been run over a couple of times by a fast truck going backwards. She's all crumpled up, got this wrecked plaid coat on looks like she slept in it. Turns out she did. In the Goodwill Box at Safeway.

"Sybilla, I feel so bad," she says, getting herself comfortable on one of my kitchen chairs. "They doing all sorts of stuff to George, got wires and tubes sticking out of his chest, won't let me get near. I'm afraid he's gonna die." And then she starts to bawl some more.

I mix up a fresh batch of Kool-Aid, try to cheer her up.

"Remember that time at Alderwood when you bit through that worker's coat?" I says.

"Yeah," she says, grinning like the old Cindy, "that dumb broad grabbed me when I wouldn't vacuum the rug."

You had to see Cindy back then. Five feet tall, about 200 pounds. And mad all the time. That shrimpy worker didn't have a chance. Getting sat on served her right. Had to go to the Hospital for shots Cindy bit her so bad. And all those workers did to Cindy was haul her off to the Therapy Room for some all-night talk about her feelings. That's all we did back then at Alderwood. Yak about feeling hostile and keep the place clean.

"Hey, Cindy," I say now, "you still feeling hostile?"

"Damned right," she says, and we laugh so hard Christian my kid comes running out from his Spiderman cartoons to see what's going on.

We remember other stuff, too. That time at Hallowe'en when she shook the ketchup bottle so hard and the lid came off and went over that worker Carlos's head. The times we snuck down to the pantry after the sleepover worker went to bed and got boxes of cookies and cans of pop if we could find where they was hid. And that crazy Alan Kamouroski finally burned down the doctor's office, used to talk in a secret language to his G.I. Joes. And Ben, the old crippled-up janitor, used to give us cigarettes if we'd show him what was in our pants.

We laugh so hard that day we have a great time.

So after that, Cindy moves in with us, eh? 'cause she's got nowheres else to go. She wants to be around in case something happens to George. But we got to be careful, got to keep our noses clean. Ever since Miss Hope, the Public Health Nurse, got the SPCA to raid this welfare dump on account of all the stray cats I keep, I'm being watched. Welfare's watching me. Miss Hope is watching me. The cops are watching me. And I know what they want but ain't ever gonna get. My kids. Christian who's nearly three and the baby, she's just turned one. They ain't ever gonna get my kids.

Last summer when they dragged away most of my cats — that Miss Hopeless said I was acting like an unfit mother. Unfit mother! What does she know? Never had a kid herself. Just this scrunched-up old broad, got wrinkles and a big fat nose, it's no wonder she's still single, no wonder at all. Not that there's much to be said for guys that knock you up then bugger off, the assholes, like them two guys did to me. Like some Indian did to Cindy, leaving her with a three-week-old baby got some kind of trouble with his lungs. Makes me figure, Cindy and me, we got to stick together, got to help each other out when we can.

It's only three months since they raided my cats, only left me with Gimp — but I'm getting more cats all the time. About four strays now and Gimp, she's about to have more babies so any day things will be back to normal.

And it turns out Cindy likes animals too. Before I know it, she's found this dog only got one eye. She was down at the dumpster at the Safeway Mall looking for extra food and this poor old thing just followed her back. We gave him a bath and he didn't look too bad but he smelled. Boy did he smell. From some kind of sores on his back. I wanted to take him to the vet but, as usual, my welfare money had run out and I couldn't borrow from Cindy, she'd just about used up all the money she brought from the reserve and the special money she got from welfare. So we just gave the dog a bath every day and fed him warm milk and crunchies.

One thing I wish is I was smart enough to have a lot of money so's I could have a clinic like that nun had looking after all the stray, sick things. I don't know why but all the animals come to me like somehow they know Sybilla's here to care. They just show up at my kitchen door needing help and I take them in. Now if only these busybody social workers and nurses would get off my back, I could get on with my important work.

But anywho, back to Cindy. Every day she hitches a ride to the hospital and every night she comes back and cries. They tell her George is still being sick and Cindy's sure he might not make it. When she tells me this I start to bawl too and grab for Christian and the baby and hold them tight. After a few days of this, things get pretty gloomy. Not only that, but things get pretty hungry, too. I hate to say this about my best friend, but Cindy eats like a horse. Ate all of Christian's Froot Loops in only one day. Eats bread and jam all the time and is always opening up cans of soup. I have to start to hide stuff when she's out so's me and the kids can get something to eat.

So one morning I finally says to her, "Jesus, Cindy, we got to do something," 'cause I'm thinking next she'll be eating the cat's crunchies and I'm beginning to feel more pissed off at her about the food than sorry for her about George.

But Cindy thinks I mean only about George and she says, "Yeah, Sybilla, maybe we should steal him right outa the hospital, bring him here for you to work on."

At first I think she's fooling but she's getting this kind of light all over her face and she's acting all happy and excited for the first time in days so I know she's really serious.

Then I'm thinking, Jesus, what am I gonna do now? I ain't ever worked on a baby sick like George before. I mean, I know what I'm doing with my cats and my dogs but a baby like George? Shit, I mean, what if we bring him here and he croaks? What would Miss Hopeless and the rest of them do to me then? And my kids. They'd be grabbing my kids for sure then.

So now I figure I got a problem and that problem is Cindy. But no way can you change Cindy's mind when she's got it made up. She'll just scream at you and call you a useless fuck and maybe even punch you in the head. I've seen her do it hundreds of times at Alderwood. She's strong and can really hurt when she wants to. Hard to believe her real name is Cinderella when she acts like that.

So I go along with her and we make up this plan, eh? about how we're gonna steal George, 'cause I figure somewheres along the way I can make things turn out different. I don't want to let on I'm scared shitless so I get all dressed up like I mean business. Got these black high-heel boots I found at the Sally Ann and this short jean skirt. Got this man's big red sweater and wear all my necklaces. It's a crime the stuff people throw away. Like all my beautiful necklaces. You have to pay five bucks at Shoppers Drug Mart just for one of them. Me, I can pick them up for 25 cents each down at the Sally Ann or St. Vincent de Paul's. I just about can't believe that they're even for sale. I mean, how could anyone throw them out? I mean, they're practically diamonds and people throw them out like they was junk!

But anywho, back to the trip. I dress my kids up, too. Christian's got on his blue suit and bow tie, what I got him for his Sears Portrait. The baby's in her pink, frilly dress. Only thing she's needing is shoes 'cause it's raining out. So I put two extra pairs of socks on her and hope she don't get cold.

I fix up Cindy, too. Try to spike her hair but it's too heavy and don't spike too good. So we settle on a pony tail and eye makeup and pink lipstick. She looks pretty good when I'm through. I can't do nothing with her clothes, though. She's too fat to fit into mine. So she just wears her jeans and the same old plaid coat.

So then we head out the door, eh? and I get scared all over again. We're walking down the street and I'm going, Jesus, I'll bet all these neighbours around here are probably staring at us like we was some crazy parade. I'll bet they're almost knowing what we're up to. We even got the one-eyed dog following us. And then I'm thinking, this is all these jerks around here is needing, another big deal to get excited about like when the SPCA raided my cats.

So we keep walking down the street out of this subdivision and heading for the highway and I'm looking around at the ticky-boo yards and all the cars and boats and trailers parked in the driveways. Me, I got to hitch a ride everywheres, there's no buses out here. But these people, I'm thinking, they got everything and yet they're always complaining about my cats, giving me all this trouble. They got all their stuff and their nice houses, you'd think that'd be enough for them, but oh no, they can't leave Sybilla alone, got to have her ass, too.

So anywho, we head out to the highway. Cindy's not saying too much and I'm still hoping she'll change her mind about stealing George. Christian, he's skipping beside us having a great time like it was Christmas. The baby, she's hanging off my hip. As usual.

Once we get to the highway it takes a while to get a ride and we start to get frozen but finally a muscle car stops. Got this one guy inside with a moustache and grinning like a loonie thinking he's shit-hot. Cindy and Christian get in the back. Me and the baby, in the front.

So this guy goes, "Where you ladies heading?" And then he revs his engine, makes it sound like it's gonna explode, makes the baby scream.

"Just give us a ride to the hospital, will ya?" I go and he looks at us strange and says like he's worried, "What's the matter?"

This makes me feel okay, like maybe here's a guy thinks of other stuff besides that thing between his legs.

So I says, "Naw, everything's all right. We're just gonna visit Cindy's baby, got sick, he's staying up the hospital."

Then he revvs his engine again and we take off. And I'm thinking, I hope Cindy got that part about us visiting George. I didn't say "stealing" him, I said *visiting*. Next thing I know this guy's passing out cigarettes, Menthol Light, and now I'm thinking, what kind of a guy smokes Menthol Light? Maybe he's weird or something, maybe he's a case.

So then this guy says to me, "Your kids?" meaning Christian and the baby.

"Yeah," I says and can't think of nothing else to say so keep quiet. But this guy's looking at my crossed legs every chance he gets, doesn't think I'm noticing but Sybilla notices just about everything. I know pretty soon he's gonna put the make on me and he's not half-bad looking either. What I'm not sure of is, do I want him to?

Nice car though. Must have cost a mint. Pretty soon he's put in a tape, some heavy metal rock, and this makes Christian jump up and down in the back seat. Me, I'm smiling to myself, suddenly having a good time — never mind the Menthol Lights — and turn around to look at Christian and then I look at Cindy and remember what it is we're gonna do. What a downer. Now I'm feeling all twisted again.

So I says to this guy, "Would you turn down the music?" 'cause I'm feeling all edgy now and he does and I'm like Thank-you, and next thing I know we're at the hospital driveway. We all get out and he drives off in a big hurry leaving rocks flying everywheres. So much for the big romance. One rock hits me in the knee and it starts to bleed like anything.

Oh great, I'm going, now we'll have to go to Emergency for a band-aid and then I go, yeah, maybe that is great. I mean, now, maybe I can stall for time.

So there we are, all heading up the hospital driveway and me, I'm limping like I was crippled, try to give the baby to Cindy to carry but she won't go. And I'm sure hoping that Emergency Room is full when we get there and have to wait for hours to get me fixed. Then maybe Cindy will forget all about stealing George and we can just have a nice visit and then go home.

But no such luck. The Emergency Room is empty. Cindy decides to go on up to the second floor to see George and wait for us there.

So Christian, the baby and me, we go into Emergency and this nurse takes the gravel junk out of my knee and puts on a band-aid. And all the while she's asking us questions like how old are the kids and what are their names. She's being so nice to us, I just about can't believe it. And everything's so white and clean and safe in there I suddenly feel like I could lie down and go to sleep and have this nurse look after me and the kids forever.

But natch, it don't go like that and we gotta say goodbye and try to find the elevator to George and Cindy. We find it all right but the problem is there's this Gift Shop right next to it and Christian, he wants to go in, have a look around. They got all kinds of neat stuff in there like little dolls with knitted dresses, I'd love one of them. And chocolate bars and magazines and two old ladies with grey hair and pink blouses making a big fuss over the baby. And I'm thinking, this Hospital sure is nice. I could stay here forever. But what I'm really thinking is, I don't want to go up and steal George and so I'm stalling anyways I can. But finally, the only thing I can figure to do, eh, is to tell Cindy what I'm thinking, like how they taught us at Alderwood, and hope she don't get too twisted. Leastways I'm figuring she won't try to bite me or something right in broad daylight, there in the Hospital.

So we get in the elevator and go up to the second floor. Soon as the door opens we see Cindy standing in front of this big glass window and she don't say nothing when we get to her but grin at us and then point to George in one of them plastic baby beds.

Finally she says, "They took the wires offa George. We don't have to steal him now. They gonna let me feed him."

And then she starts to bawl and me, I start bawling, too, not only for being happy about George, not only that. I'm bawling because now I don't have to do nothing about making him better. Now I don't have to do all the worrying about is he gonna die.

So we leave Cindy, eh? She's gonna hang around till two when she can give George his bottle. Christian and me and the baby, we go down to the Gift Shop, get three chocolate bars to celebrate. George is gonna be okay and me and Cindy, we can go back to being best friends like before.

We head out of the hospital and into the rain, happier than three pigs in shit, and we're hardly out of the building when all of a sudden that muscle car pulls up, got the same guy inside. He hangs his head out the window and says, "Wanna ride?" and me, I'm getting a big thrill now thinking this guy's been waiting for us, thinking why not?, ain't this something? Maybe finally here's a guy who ain't an asshole, maybe here's a guy who'll care.

So we get in, eh? and I'm like "Thank you, you can give us a lift" and I slam the door and he says, smiling really nice, "Where to?" and hands me a Menthol Light and then me and Christian and the baby, we take off with him down the highway, rocks flying everywheres, like nobody's business.

ROB'S GUNS & AMMO

There's this old guy, maybe forty, forty-five got this business in town? I figure he's my Dad. I mean, he looks like me. Small. Skinny. Got the same pointy nose. Only difference his hair is brown and mine's blonde. Well, yellow really. But the roots, they'd be about the same.

It'd be real easy to prove we was related. Just stand us side by side. Just stand us together in front of a mirror. I mean, any idiot would have to say, "Yeah, Sybilla, he's gotta be your Dad. No doubt about it." I mean, shit, we could be twins if he wasn't such an old fart.

And the name's right, too. Rob. Says so right on his sign. ROB'S GUNS & AMMO. Is that proof or what?

Well, all right, maybe I don't know for sure he's my Dad. I mean, my Mom, all she ever told me before she died was his name. But I've been putting two and two together. His name and how he looks — plus where I was born, only twenty miles from here — and coming up with one, big happy family. Which is about time. After all those years in Alderwood, that treatment centre I was in for screwed-up kids.

So don't laugh, asshole. Is it my fault my Mom was a drunk and I got taken away? Gimme a break.

Eight years old and thrown in a treatment centre. You'd be disturbed, too, after going through that. I mean, that place was like a prison. All we ever did there was clean the floors. Do the dishes. What they called "functioning". And talk about our feelings. Talk about our feelings *to death*.

Don't ever ask me how I'm feeling. Don't ever say those words to me. I'm likely to go strange on you. I must of sat at the kitchen table at Alderwood a thousand times having to *talk about my feelings*. Having to explain why I figured some worker was a douche-bag. Why some other kid deserved to have her Barbie doll swiped. Over and over. It never stopped, that talking. Every time I'd turn around some worker would be on my case. *How do you feel about* this, *Sybilla? How do you feel about* that, *Sybilla?* It got so's the sound of those words made me wanna puke. And when I was thirteen and a half and ran away for the last time? What did my Social Worker lay on me but, *"How do you feel about going to a group home, Sybilla?"*

Feelings. It's like some disease all these workers got. Even Miss Hope, the Public Health Nurse always banging on my door? Checking up on germs and corruption? She's a feeling freak, too. "How does it *feel*, Sybilla, to be on Welfare?"

"Oh terrific," I go, thinking you dumb broad, how do you think it *feels*? It feels like shit. Shitty. The pits.

But is she satisfied with that? No way. She's got to go for the throat. "No really, Sybilla, how does it *really* make you *feel*?"

Lights all flashing like this was some TV quiz show and I get the big prize if I answer right. Like stars on the fridge at Alderwood. Tokens. Ten tokens gets you a chocolate bar. But first you gotta say the right words about your feelings. First you gotta slobber after their praise.

A hundred tokens gets you taken to a movie by your favourite worker. That's a laugh! I mean, who'd ever have a favourite worker? That's like having a favourite spider. Or poisonous snake.

So I'm up to here with all these yo-yo's. With all their talk. They're paid to do that. Ask about your *feelings*. Pretend they care. I figure it's time I had my own family. I mean, besides Christian and the baby. I figure it's time I got my Dad to take care of me the way he should a done all those years ago.

Only thing is, first I gotta convince this guy Rob he's my Dad.

So every time we stand out front ROB'S GUNS & AMMO I says to Christian, look Christian, see that man in there? He's probably your Grandpa.

And Christian, who's three, he gets all excited jumps up and down starts waving his arms the way he did last Christmas at Santa Claus in the parade.

Which isn't far off. Santa Claus, I mean. I figure Rob's gotta be rich. Having a store like that. He's gotta be loaded. The stuff in the two big windows for starters. Megabucks. Stuff for hunting and fishing. Basketball hoops. Expensive running shoes like what the sports stars wear on TV. Hats. And all kinds of junk for camping. Stoves. Sleeping bags hanging off the ceiling.

With all the money Rob's got he could start me a kennel so's I don't have all my animals in the house no more. Causing Miss Hopeless to get all twisted about the smell every time she barges in for a visit. You'd think she was my best friend or something. All the time she spends with us. Getting me to clean up the place just like you-know-where.

"I'm too busy," I go. "I got all these animals to look after."

But she's always talking at me. Yak. Yak. Yak. About the baby's Pampers, are they changed enough? About keeping stuff off the floor so's Christian and the baby don't put dirt in their mouths and get diarrhea.

"Get me a kennel," I go, "then there won't be dirt on the floor. Or get Welfare to get me a decent house. Get all these jerks I got for neighbours off my back, then we can talk about dirt on the floor."

So I figure having Rob for my Dad would end all the hassle. It's the perfect solution. That's why we hang around his store so much. Nearly every day. Getting up the nerve to go in and introduce ourselves.

Only problem is, how do I do it? I mean, we're total strangers to him, right? Do I march in the store and say, "Hi there, remember way back when? . . . a girl called Rita? . . . that was my mother . . . well, you knocked her up . . ."

Sure I'm gonna say that. Get real. That sounds like I'm some nut case out on a day pass. Like I'm brain-damaged.

Or how 'bout: "Hey Rob, ever wonder if you had a kid someplace you didn't know about?"

Ha! What kind of a guy is gonna own up to that?

So that's why I been chickenshit about going in, eh? I mean, how do I start a conversation? How do I prove to him he's my Dad? How do I tell him about us so he won't say *fuck off asshole*? He could just say I'm crazy, get outa here, get lost, who'd want you for a daugther?

This Rob, he could say anything he likes. I mean, it's really important to me he's my Dad and I don't want to scare him off.

I'd even settle for some money from him. Enough to get off Welfare and start me a kennel. And maybe a visit with him now and then. That'd be okay. You know, like at Christmas? Or my birthday?

So this Rob, he's my number one project now. Lots of times I seen him in the store. Hanging stuff on the racks. Dusting all the guns he's got in a glass case behind the counter. Helping customers. One time I saw him walking down Beacon Avenue around lunch time. Me and Christian and the baby in the stroller, we wheeled around and followed him like he was a magnet. Right into the Beacon Café. Even stood behind him in the take-out line. With my high-heeled boots on we was about the same size. He got himself a bowl of chili, two buns, a salad and a coffee. Christian and me, we split a Coke. Sat in the booth across from him but didn't have the nerve to say hello.

A couple of times he's smiled at me through the window but not like he knew me or anything. The same kind of smile he gives the guys who buy guns and fishing rods.

And I can't stop thinking about him. Rob. Like where does he live and how it'll be when he knows I'm his daughter. And all the stuff he'll give us outa the store. And all of us going to the Beacon Café for lunch. And how he's buying.

So we was going along like this for a couple of weeks. Hanging out front the store and smiling at Rob when we could see him. You know, trying to get him used to us and hoping pretty soon he'd want to meet us.

And then last Monday something really weird happened. Something that's like made the whole story a lot more interesting. For me anyways.

We was standing out front the store like usual. Killing time. Waiting to go down the Welfare Office. Our cheque was supposed to be in at ten.

The baby, she was asleep in her stroller and Christian, he had his Hot Wheels car, going vroom vroom back and forth on the window ledge. Rob, I could see him, he was inside behind the counter working at some papers.

I was just gonna say to Christian, come on Christian, I guess we stood out here long enough for one day, when out the store in a big hurry comes this fat old broad. Purple sweatsuit, frizzy grey hair. Comes right up to me.

She's got this mean look on her face and she says, "Can I help you?" Acting like she owns the place.

You got to see her. One of these sour jobs. All squished-up face like a Social Worker I had once. Doesn't take me two seconds to hate her.

So I says to her, "No thanks, we're just standing here deciding which parked car we're gonna steal." I thought it was funny.

But she didn't. She's sucking lemons. "Well," she says, "you been hanging out front the store quite a lot lately and if you don't have business here then you'd better leave."

"It's a free country," I goes, or some such garbage. "I can stand where I wants to."

So then she goes off on this big speech, eh? About how the front of the store is *her* property and how I'm tresspassing and if I want to hang out somewheres why don't I go to the park down the wharf?

And I'm looking the other way, not at her, like I used to do at Alderwood, to all the workers. Pretending I'm deaf. Acting like it's all one big gi-normous yawn till finally I gets sick of her yapping and tells her to fuck off which I probably shouldn't a done cause then she gets all twisted and red in the face and starts screaming at us right there on the street. Screaming about my *language* and what kind of mother would talk like that and how we're all alike — whatever that means — and on and on till finally I says, "Well I got a right to be here. I know Rob," figuring that would shut her up. What an idiot thing to say. Does Sybilla ever keep her trap shut? Like shoot my brains out and I still wouldn't know I was dead.

So this old bag goes, "What Rob?"

"Rob inside," I go, trying to sound as mean as she looks. "Rob who owns the store."

"I own the store," she says, "and there is no Rob. That's just the name of the store when I bought it."

"Yeah sure," I go, "well who's that?" and I'm pointing past her through the window.

So this old broad turns around has herself a look, eh? Then she laughs, a snarly kind of laugh. "That's Earl," she says. "Earl who works for me. What you want with Earl?"

"Don't give me that shit," I says 'cause I don't believe her one bit and then Christian starts bawling and grabbing at my leg. "Now look what you've done," I'm shouting. "You've scared my kid. I could get the cops after you for child abuse, you know, frightening little kids."

And I picks Christian up to make it look good and by now people are slowing down and stopping on the sidewalk, having a look at us.

The old bag turns around then shaking her head and storms back in the store. Slams the door so hard the little bell comes crashing onto the sidewalk. And the people who was watching us? After a few minutes, they just kind of melt away.

Then I'm just like Christian, I can't stop bawling. Standing there on the sidewalk out front of Rob's store I'm bawling like an idiot. Everything's got so mixed up. Everything's got so crazy.

So the only thing I can figure to do, eh? is stay standing there till I'm good and ready to leave. No old bag is gonna scare me off, I'm thinking. No douche-bag pushes Sybilla around and gets away with it.

So we stand there for maybe another fifteen minutes just to make our point. Don't even turn around and look in the store window though I can tell the old bag is gunning me, watching every move I make.

And when we finally start heading down Beacon Avenue it's because I want to. Not because we've been told to leave. It's because it's ten by now and our cheque's in down at the Welfare Office.

So that's where we go next, eh? Get my cheque then head over to the pet store to get it cashed. So what if I blew it all on fish? Well, nearly all of it. That's my business.

Tropical fish. And all the junk that goes with them. The tank. Food. Little castles that go in the tank. And special white rocks that come in a plastic bag. I got six of them. We got so much stuff we had to take a taxi home.

So it's four days later and we're still hanging out front ROB'S GUNS & AMMO. I figure that old bag was lying to me. About Rob being Earl. About it being *her* store. About everything. She's got it in for me, that I know for sure. And I still figure Rob's my Dad. It won't be long before he figures it out, too. Then everything'll be okay. Don't ask me how I know this. I just do.

So far the old bag hasn't hassled us no more but I seen her peeking at us a couple of times. From behind a rack of ski jackets. And Rob, I still see him every day. Not paying much attention to us. Working away in his store.

A couple of times a cop car has gone by real slow, having a good look at us standing out front. Hasn't done nothing yet. And Miss Hopeless the other day? She asks me how come I was hanging around Rob's so much. But do I talk to workers? Do I spill my guts for free? You already know the answer to that one.

So it's giving me a big laugh. I mean, all these people hovering around — the cops, Miss Hopeless, the old bag — they're just like the fish in my new tank. Doing all this quiet cruising. Day after day. Just waiting to see what old Sybilla's gonna do next. Holding their breaths, all nervous, in case I go strange on them.

But maybe you think I'm cracked, eh? All this stuff about Rob being my Dad? Well, all I got to say about that is: blow it out your ear. I'm like one of my dogs with a bone when I know a thing for sure. I won't ever let go of it no matter what. No one's gonna change my mind about Rob. Not in a million years. Not ever. So don't even try.

THE LONELIEST SOUND YOU'LL EVER HEAR

Jimmy Silvey rides the range. This time he's in a bar drinking alone, the tall, rumpled-looking man in the corner by the pool table watching three Indian women. They wear different combinations of black and purple like a bruise and give Jimmy Silvey quick, sharp looks that are not meant to be noticed. He nurses his beer, pretending to ignore them, and listens to their conversation. Mostly they are saying what a bastard some guy called Lewis is and then they begin a game of pool. They take a long time choosing their pool cues, all the while pulling at their sweaters like some kind of signal and blowing cigarette smoke out of their nostrils like mad horses. Jimmy takes the one in the middle, the fat one, not usually chosen, Carol-Ann. And leaves her somewhere in northern Alberta before the child comes.

Another time. Coming home to his mother's dump after two years of wandering. Wheeling his ruined blue pick-up off the ferry and out into the cool grey drizzle, his aged dog wheezing on the seat beside him, her old tail wagging as soon as they hit the coast and Jimmy Silvey, bringing his dog home to die and himself home to rest a while.

He can see himself in his lone truck, rainwater flying up from the wheels as he crests the quiet town below, the lone stranger riding through the deserted October streets, a silent man out of nowhere and with nothing but the contents of his saddle bag, a sensitive man with a dying dog and an old mother, with his collar turned up and his baseball cap pulled low against the big thoughts eating up his brain and the small adventures squeezing out his soul, riding into town on this desolate Sunday morning, the only sounds, the rain splatting his tires, his wheezing dog, the suck of his cigarette.

To plead his case. Only that his soul is a boiling black cloud that won't be stayed, a train that's moving on. Away but never to a thing. The smooth, vacant road, he says, it calls, he's got to wander. The loneliest sound you'll ever hear is the wind high up in the cold firs that line Jimmy Silvey's road, is the thin, distant cry from Carol-Ann in the bare motel room, her heart slowly tearing.

Ultimately the heart. The heart of Jimmy Silvey, his reason why. He cannot answer the question precisely, never having had any luck in this world. Cheerless drifter. Blown like dust before the wind, whirlpools of ugly emotions, blown by his own restless soul across arid landscapes, through empty, haunting forests. To land in dry unexpected places. Moving on.

At times to his mother. Having lost all sense of him, year after year, never knowing when he'll turn up. Jimmy Silvey parks his truck on the wet grass in front of his mother's house and quiets the dog who has struggled to sit up, a look of expectation on her face. A large heavy dog, her face covered with white hairs, her tail thumping on the ripped vinyl seat.

The same old house. Grey stucco walls, wet concrete steps, the wooden front door. The soggy poverty of the place. And the garden, too, drowned: a ragged chrysanthemum, a small drooping bush. Jimmy Silvey imagines the lonely woman inside, her life sodden with boredom, imagines his mere ruined presence bringing joy, like an unexpected gift.

This time she's at the kitchen counter buttering toast. Jimmy Silvey comes up behind her, quiet as a cat, and calls her name so softly she thinks it is her own sad desire speaking to her. But there he surely is, her own poor Jimmy, never having had any luck in this world. He is thinner than she remembers, his clothes dirty, the smell of him strong like gasoline, sour like sweat, and thinning on the top she notices and sagging beneath the eyes as if his whole face was hollowing in. Home at last and doesn't he look as if he needs someone to love him?

Then the dog. Jimmy Silvey helps her out of the truck. His mother, wrapped now in a cardigan against the forlorn morning, is with him too, offering the dog pieces of buttered toast. "Who's a good dog now?" she's saying, stroking the bony back, kissing the old dog on the head. "Who's a good old thing?"

We're all she has, Jimmy thinks, and feels the weight of that responsibility descend upon him like an angry black cloud, feels the storm it causes in his heart whenever he cannot give what is needed.

He stays the winter. To rest a while. With his dog and his mother, the only beings in Jimmy Silvey's world who love him without question, without reason.

And then it's spring. Jimmy Silvey spends the last two weeks of April working on the truck's transmission out in his mother's driveway. The world suddenly a brighter place, everything alive around him: flowers, birds, dogs, kids on bikes, pensioners pulling at weeds in their derelict gardens, all of them shaking off the soggy winter, putting hopeful faces towards the sun and taking deep breaths of the sudden sweet air and smiling.

And Jimmy Silvery's heart fills with the same impulse of hope and his thoughts turn towards Alberta and Carol-Ann and the baby. He plays the truck radio as he works and his soul, it seems to swell as he listens to the music, some rock and roll tune about love and good times. And he gets an idea. A golden idea that's pulling him away from the dreary time with his mother, now that he's rested. Some bright dream scene about things being all right with Carol-Ann. He can almost see himself happy, riding into that northern Alberta town to see her, arriving like a surprise out of nowhere and the brightness he might possibly bring. Having dreamed up the next place to go.

And so on the first Monday in May he loads into the truck his wheezing dog who did not die and kisses his sad mother good-bye and heads out towards the ferry, impatient to be on his way and thinking of Carol-Ann and the child, she must be two by now, and wondering if they are still at the same motel or if they have moved or if he can find them.

Time passes. Jimmy Silvey wanders the range, a drifter along Route 401. His truck, broken down, is left for dead by the side of the road, his dog buried in a ditch along the way. Carol-Ann is from another time.

A man of few words, he hitches rides, does odd jobs, sleeping roadside when it's warm, on floors during winter. Surprising no one. Jimmy's eyes are rigid pools finding a point and moving towards it. His heart is an empty husk blown on its stubborn way.

Alone in the mountains for two weeks, Jimmy Silvey hears a train whistle. The loneliest sound you'll ever hear, he thinks. It sounds like a thin, distant cry. He walks towards it furtively, fists clenched at his side. Deliberately through rough salal, slippery ravines, over rotting logs. It's a bright sunlit morning yet he seems to wander under the cover of night, in fear, watching the vacant forest for signs of his personal doom: murderers with guns, knives, ravaging animals, the sudden upheaval of old timber.

He wears his hair slicked back beneath a baseball cap, a cheap brown suit tied at the waist with a rope. Carries a slender pack over his shoulders, covers his eyes with large wrap-around sun glasses, disguising himself against the treachery without, the emptiness within. Jimmy Silvey is hurrying through every obstacle towards that crying sound, a man, for the moment, with someplace to go.

SIDE BY SIDE

Your husband's eyes are mild brown behind his glasses; the fringe around his bald head is black and grey. He's always sucking a hard candy, lips full and puckered. The candy he is sucking now is green, his favourite.

You're on your hands and knees scrubbing the linoleum on the kitchen floor. A cigarette sticks out the side of your mouth, the ash, a good two inches in length, threatens to fall on the shiny, wet floor.

Your husband says, "Why are you bothering to wash and wax the floor? Nobody will even come in here."

"Little do you know," you say. The importance of clean floors, like babies and cooking hams, is remote to him. You're hosting a Sunday supper on your front patio. There are pies to make. Pies and more pies. They are remote to him as you are.

Your husband cleans his glasses with his handkerchief. He shakes his head. You've been married for thirty-one years. He shakes his head, dismissing your effort. It's the only criticism you ever get but it covers everything.

There are three pies: one cherry, one raisin, one apple. Just out of the oven, they sit, side by side on the arborite kitchen table, on display. The cherry pie has a lattice cover, criss-crossed strands of pastry sprinkled with sugar. The raisin pie has a pastry "R", the apple pie, a pastry "A".

Also on the table are two bowls of potato chips, one smooth, one crinkled, and an onion-flavoured chip dip in a cut glass bowl. There is a bowl of Cheesies, too, because your brother Eddy is fond of these.

The ham is in the oven. Maudie is bringing the potato salad. Your brother's wife, you note grimly, is bringing the buns, one dozen white, one dozen brown. Grandma, your mother, is not bringing anything because now it is your turn.

You count who is coming, making sure you have the right number of plates — thirteen.

You want the day to be nice. The high, white summer haze you can see from your kitchen window is a worry.

"Put those chairs on the patio out of the wind," you say to your husband who's taking the kitchen chairs outside. "Nobody wants to sit in the cold and have their napkins blown about. You know how Grandma hates a draft."

None of your husband's family are coming to the supper. This is just fine with you.

Grandma stands at the end of Maudie's driveway to wait for the ride to the supper. She always waits at the end of the driveway for the rides, no matter where she is going: to pick up groceries, to visit the graves of her husband and son-in-law. Maudie doesn't drive. If it happens to be raining, she'll stand under cover of the front porch. Grandma is eighty-six years old and deaf.

She carries her black handbag over the stump of her right arm (amputated fifteen years ago after a fall in the snow). Her good arm is shielding her eyes from the sun as she peers up the road towards the approaching car. Your husband has arrived.

Maudie, your widowed sister, hurries out of the house, locking the front door and the garage door, even though her son, Larry, is asleep inside. She hurries towards the car. She, too, has a black handbag and is carrying a large glass bowl covered with Saran Wrap, the potato salad. She is smiling.

Your husband says, "Why'd you lock all the doors for if Larry is asleep inside? Afraid someone will steal him?"

Your husband takes another look at Larry's hot rod parked out front of the house and mumbles, "Lazy bugger."

Driving off, Maudie looks out of your husband's back seat window at her son's car and smiles.

Grandma says, "Eh?"

Everyone, except Larry, arrives while your husband is out. Three extra cars are parked in the driveway at odd angles. You know your husband will be annoyed that he wasn't back in time to direct traffic.

When Grandma arrives she says to you in the kitchen, "I knew we'd be late," even though it is only three o'clock in the afternoon.

Standing at the kitchen table, staring down at the food, she drags one finger across the onion chip dip. "Too salty," she announces.

Maudie puts her potato salad in your fridge; you're basting the ham.

"Need any help?" she asks.

"Not now," you say, "maybe with the serving, when it's time to eat."

Outside your son-in-law opens a cooler full of beer. He gives one to your brother Eddy. Your husband doesn't drink anything. He's busy shoving wire hoops into the front lawn in case anyone wants to play croquet, later on.

You're wearing your good navy-blue summer dress; your apron is smudged with pastry flour. At four o'clock you take a break from the kitchen to sit outside on the patio with Grandma and Maudie. The three of you sit in a row on the kitchen chairs placed carefully, side by side, in the shade of the house. Small women, your feet do not touch the ground. You swing your legs while you talk. Maudie sits on her hands. You look like three crows on a clothesline.

Grandma complains to you, not for the first time. "All Larry does is sleep. Won't even take out the garbage. Maudie has to."

Maudie shrugs her shoulders. If this bothers her, she's not going to say; she is known as a person who never has a harsh word to say about anyone, particularly her only child.

Not so her mother. "And playing the banjo all the time. The racket!" Grandma continues, yelling. "I have to sit in the bathroom to get any peace and quiet."

A candy-apple-red hot rod pulls into the driveway.

"Well, speak of the devil," Grandma says. "Here he is. In time for supper. As usual."

You know why Larry is the way he is: Maudie spoils him. She's been spoiling him since the day he was born. He doesn't have to lift a finger, his mother keeps him. She has her husband's generous pension from the Navy, there's never any shortage of money for Larry.

SIDE BY SIDE

You've got two daughters, they've turned out all right. Married, each with a baby. You watch them now, busy, capable girls. They've got their babies, side by side, on a blanket in the bright sun. Laughing together, they're comparing the sizes of the babies' feet. Their young husbands stare down at them from the lawn chairs, quiet boys, each one holding a can of beer.

You watch your husband. He's sixty-two, overweight, always wearing those beige work clothes, pants and shirt, winter or summer. A janitor at the Public Library. A good provider. Handy around the house. He's moving the sprinkler away from the babies' blanket. A concerned, serious man. Sometimes in front of company he calls you "dear". Once you called him "sensitive". You remember how, before you were married, he fainted in a movie. He has never liked strong emotion. You wonder if he still likes you. You've had separate bedrooms for six years.

Larry has thick, wavy blonde hair. Sometimes he lets the younger cousins, Eddy's girls, comb it. Last summer at one of your outdoor suppers, it was his idea to staple Grandma's black hat to the patio roof. Grandma got even by pouring his beer down your kitchen sink. The family still talks about this: Grandma is a character.

Before supper, Larry lounges on the lawn like it was a bed. A plastic tail-comb sticks out of the back pocket of his jeans. He's drinking his third can of beer.

Grandma yells across to him from her kitchen chair in the shade. "What you drinking that muck for?"

Larry, pretending to be deaf, cups his ear. "Eh?" he says.

"I said, 'What are you drinking that muck for?'"

Larry says, "Eh?"

Everyone laughs.

Grandma waves her hand at him. "Oh go on with ya."

Larry says, "Eh?"

A sudden wind comes up, cooling the sun.

Grandma shouts, "Maudie, Maudie. Where's my sweater?"

You say, "Chip? Chip? Anyone want a chip?" passing around the bowls of potato chips and dip.

Eddy's girls, plump 13- and 15-year-olds, lie on a car blanket on the lawn beside the patio reading romance novels, eating O'Henry bars. The wind blows a candy wrapper across the lawn; it lodges at the base of a rose bush.

For some time now the girls have been whining to their mother that there's no pop to drink, only purple Kool-Aid. Your husband offers to drive them to the corner store for Orange Crush, he's buying. As he's leaving he shakes his head and gives you a severe look: providing pop and not Kool-Aid was your department.

Grandma gets off her chair, shivering. She looks at her watch and says to you irritably, "It's five o'clock. Time for supper."

You and Maudie hurry into the house, momentarily playing the scolded daughters. You laugh together in the kitchen, peeling the Saran Wrap from the potato salad, slicing the ham.

"If looks could kill," you say of your husband, the way he looked at you just now.

Maudie shakes her head, smiling. Your older, calmer sister. She thinks you mean Grandma. "Well, she's not as young as she once was," she says, "and you know how she hates a draft."

You hate to watch your husband eat. He has a plate with a piece of pie on it, apple, his favourite. He's sitting on a kitchen chair on the patio beside Grandma, balancing the plate on his lap in mock daintiness. You know he will chew his pie with his front teeth, his back teeth give him trouble. You know that when he has finished his pie there will be flakes of pastry stuck to his shiny protruding lips. You look away, embarrassed.

If this were the two of you at supper, you'd say harshly, "Wipe your mouth, there's food all over it!" and he'd say, "Nag, nag," and leave it there. Then you wouldn't speak for days.

Grandma says of her piece of cherry pie, "Good pie."

Everyone else nods in chorus, "Good pie. Delicious."

Your husband says nothing, takes a second helping. You'll remember all of this, later on.

After supper, the women help with the dishes. You like the activity in your kitchen, the closeness of it, it's the best of times for you, everyone working together.

Grandma is drying, holding a plate under her elbow, drying it with her good arm. You feel proud of your white linen tea-towels, freshly bleached.

"I won't put these dishes away," Grandma says, "I don't know where they go." She stacks them on the kitchen table.

Maudie says, "What do you want to do with this left-over potato salad?"

You tell her to take it home.

She seems pleased. "It will do for Larry's lunch tomorrow," she says.

You and your daughters exchange looks: it's hard to imagine Larry getting up before two.

Grandma, who is known to hear when she wants to, says, "Lunch! That'll be the day. All he ever does is sleep."

After the dishes are done you serve tea and coffee on the patio. The wind, you are relieved to find, has died down; the air is calm, pleasant. Eddy's girls slouch in deck chairs, sighing, looking bored. It is your opinion that if they helped a little now and then they might find things more interesting. For example, they could have helped with the dishes just now instead of acting like Queen Bees, lounging on the patio with the men. You would have never allowed your girls to behave like that.

Larry brings out his banjo from the trunk of his car and starts to tune it, humming quietly.

Eddy's girls perk up. One says, "Play something. Oh please."

Eddy starts to play "Side By Side", Grandma's favourite.

Standing in the doorway, you gaze down upon your family gathered together, listening to Larry sing, not too loudly because it is out of doors, but singing just the same.

At seven o'clock, Larry takes his mother and his grandmother home. His hot rod is lowered to six inches at the front, it only has a forward seat. Grandma sits primly in the middle of this one and only seat, her black handbag on her lap, her black hat just visible behind the fuzzy dice which hang from Larry's rear-view mirror. Beside her, from the passenger seat, Maudie laughs and waves a handkerchief like she was going on a world cruise. Larry revs the engine. He revs it three, four times, then, with tires squealing, lays rubber as he pulls out of your driveway onto the main road.

Even when they are out of sight, you can hear Larry's tires squealing in the distance. You laugh a little to imagine Grandma in the front seat, her head pulled back from the speed. You shake your head and wonder what she'll have to say about all of this, later on.

After supper, when everyone has left, you make yourself a cup of tea and sit on the front patio to relax. You light a cigarette. Your husband has already put the kitchen chairs back in the house; he's got the TV on, you can hear the muted sounds, a comedy show of some sort, you can hear the staccato sounds of laughter.

It's still light out. You look with pleasure at your neatly-trimmed lawn, at the border of yellow chrysanthemums putting on such a show, at the Peace rose, in bloom. A quiet, contented yard.

Smiling now, you think of your grandchildren, of the new pleasant strangeness you feel at being a grandmother. You're looking forward to the autum and the knitting you will do then.

You finish your cigarette and head towards the house. Reaching the front door you wonder how many grandchildren you'll eventually have. Four, at least, you decide.

THE BIBLE IN LONGHAND

Robert sits on the bed in his room. A small, slight man, he wears a maroon toque, brown pants, a heavy woollen sweater. It is late spring.

He has stuck a long piece of cotton wool in each ear, the wool hangs to his shoulders like drooping antennae. He wears it in his ears at all times, even while he sleeps (which is not often) because he wants to stop the strange noises from entering his brain. But sometimes a voice will suffuse his cotton wool, beginning at his shoulder and creeping upwards like water through a sponge, so that the cotton wool becomes laden with strange sounds which seep into his outer ears. From there the noises swirl down his ear canals like water down a drainpipe to finally explode into his brain and torment him with terrible commands. He has to check the cotton wool frequently for voices.

When Robert removes it from his ears he hears nothing, however, but the pounding of his heart. Then the low rumble of his mother's refrigerator.

For no reason at all a bird lands outside his windowsill like a warning. "Spring is for death. Spring is for death," it screams, then splits in half.

Robert is thirty-five years old. He has stayed in his room for seven years. He only comes out to go to the bathroom or to feed himself at the kitchen counter. He eats only the insides of things: the centre circle of a slice of bread, a piece of meat, the inside of an apple. Water has to run out of the tap a long time before he will drink it.

Before Robert can leave his room there are certain things that he must do: he must secure the tinfoil around the perimeter of his window, make sure that his bedcovers are securely tucked in, and check the corners of his walls for cracks. Once a spider came through, breathing fire.

It is his boyhood room. He still has the cowboy bedspread on his bed. A model airplane is allowed to stay on his dresser and guard the room in his absence.

Robert stands at the kitchen counter to eat his meals, the cotton wool in his ears, the maroon toque on his head, a grey blanket draped over his shoulders. He eats furtively, rabbit-like. He does not want food in his room. Crumbs could grow into giant living things, pulsating like raw hearts, ready to devour him.

While he eats, his mother peeks at him from behind the kitchen door.

From his room, Robert hears a human voice. Three voices. His mother's and his father's and a third, unknown voice. He hears their worried sounds, whining like a musical saw. Then he hears his mother say, "This way, Doctor."

They are going to divide me up, Robert thinks, they've sent someone to break me up, cell by cell, and scatter my parts so that I will never be whole again.

He locks himself in the bathroom, flushes the toilet and runs the sink water so that he cannot hear the pounding on the door. It's a hollow pounding like the roar from a distant canyon.

Robert stays in the bathroom a long time, until he hears the doctor leave. Then he worries about his room, he had not prepared to leave it.

Inspecting it when he finally returns, he finds a tear in his tinfoil, his model airplane has melted. And then a voice invades his chest, screaming, "Smash the glass. Smash the glass."

Robert goes into the kitchen, picks up a chair and takes it into the living room. His mother is knitting, something blue, his father lies asleep on the couch. Robert throws the chair through the living room window; it sends shards of glass flying at his parents like deliberate missiles. A piece of glass slices open his mother's hand, her blood pours onto her blue knitting. It looks to Robert as if her veins are long wool-like threads and her blood lives outside her body.

He screams but no sound comes from his mouth.

Robert's father telephones a relative who is a social worker. They meet secretly over coffee at a department store, this is not an official visit.

The father wants to go on a trip to Portugal but the mother won't leave Robert. What can he do?

"Have him committed," says the relative.

"I couldn't," says the father, "it would break his mother's heart."

"Seven years is a long time to stay in your room," says the relative and then suggests that if the father is not prepared to force help on Robert then they had all just better live with it.

"I feel trapped in my own house," the father complains. "The plans I had when I retired."

"Then do something," says the relative.

"I can't," says the father.

"What if he gets violent again?"

"He never has before this," the father says. "In seven years, the living-room window has been the only time . . . But maybe his brother could help. They were always so close. I'll write to his brother."

Robert calls his mother Barbara and his father Jack. He sees them sometimes in the kitchen or passes them on his way to the bathroom.

They walk around on short stick legs, their hair is the colour of ashes, their mouths are obscene red holes.

When they speak, words rise in bubbles and drift towards the kitchen ceiling, where they break like waves against a shore to form a slow, grey fog. To Robert this fog is a sign of death. He watches it seep into his parents' ears, soon it will find their elderly hearts and claim them. Soon they will disappear into the fog and cease to exist.

His parents huddle outside Robert's door and whisper. Their bubble words find their way through his wall and catch him on the side of the head. But do not turn to fog. Instead they stick to him like clown balloons and when they finally break they leave four words exposed and hovering in the air: "Jackie is coming home."

Soon after, Robert has a dream. A voice finds itself a germ and becomes a cavity in his tooth. It seems the invaders have a new tactic: they will rot him from the inside using his teeth as pathways.

Awake, Robert leaves his room and finds a telephone book on the kitchen counter. He looks up the number of a taxi company, the address of a dentist, and his own address, since he has forgotten it. He makes a phone call, uttering his first sentence in seven years: "Come to 4921 Wilkinson Road."

For the trip Robert wears his gloves, his toque, the cotton wool and his father's topcoat. When the doorbell rings he hears his mother say, "Who can that be?" and then sees her gape, astonished, as he strides past her and out the door, carrying the telephone book.

On the walkway to the taxi Robert is surprised to find that his feet stay on the ground. He feels like a balloon, any minute now he will float away into the vast outside, into the throbbing greenness.

The taxi driver's face is a brown question mark covered in oil. "Where to?" he asks, opening the back door of the taxi.

Robert gets in and instantly feels safe. "Surrounded by metal," he says.

"Where to?" the driver repeats.

Robert points to a name in the telephone book. He has chosen a Doctor David Dark. He liked all the solid "D's" sitting on the page like army tanks.

Barbara and Jack peer out from behind the living room curtains, wearing their grey fog, nervous like small, grey mice.

As Robert rides, drops of water full of invaders hit the car, then dribble down the side of the window, defeated. Robert remembers about rain: it is raining outside. Touching his coat, he can feel the slight dampness.

"Got a sore ear?" the driver calls from the front seat as they glide along the oily streets, safe in their metal capsule.

Looking out the window, Robert sees the grey and white houses join hands and grin.

The taxi stops outside a building. Robert sees countless people crowded onto the sidewalk like writhing insects, sees everywhere skin, everywhere shadow. The drops of water do not seem to bother them.

"When the water stops," he says to the driver.

"That'll be the day. Here, you can use my umbrella. I'll wait for you."

Inside the building Robert hears the walls creaking and human voices but nothing else. It is safe in here, too, he decides.

When he finally finds Dr. Dark's office, a woman in white with a large red face says, "But you don't have an appointment," and hands him a green card. "Come back on the 9th," she says.

Back in the taxi, Robert hands the card to the driver. "Come and get me," he says.

At home, Robert gets out of the taxi, walks through the front door and shuts himself in his bedroom. His father pays the taxi fare.

Barbara says to Jackie, her other son: "He always was an awkward, oddish boy . . . Perhaps that summer in '62 at camp, the unkind boys . . . Or perhaps the time you took his model planes and sold them down the street . . . Or maybe it was he failed three years at the university and then he failed at love... He cut his wrists but did not die... Or maybe seven years ago those shocks to his brain at Riverview... The leather stool he made for your Dad then later carved to bits...

Robert is sitting on his bed listening to the slow even beats of his heart. One thousand. Two thousand. Once pieces of his heart hung like shredded scabs from the branches of a ghastly tree and each piece was his lady's song. One thousand times his heart was ripped by that ghastly call: "Good-bye, Robert... Goodbye..."

There is a knock at his door and then it is opened.

"Hi!" says a voice from a body, large as the doorway. "It's me, Jackie, your brother. I've brought you a present."

Jackie puts the parcel on the bed beside Robert. It is a square, soft parcel wrapped in white paper and tied with a red ribbon. The parcel looks like a Red Cross flag.

Robert stares at Jackie. His eyes blink turtle-slow.

"So what's new?" Jackie asks.

Robert counts silently to one thousand, then answers, "I went to the dentist but he wasn't there."

"Oh."

One thousand. Two thousand. Jackie leaves.

Robert slowly opens the parcel. Two magazines. One *Playboy*. One *Penthouse*.

Weeks pass. The magazines remain unopened on the bed; Robert sleeps on the floor to avoid touching them.

The satiny magazine covers glow radium-green in the night. Robert knows what they contain: the seeds of soft Ophelia, each seed aching to find his heart and grow there, each seed aching to grow throny branches to tear at his heart.

Now his heart is pounding. He yearns to forget his heart.

A ring at the doorbell, the waiting taxi. Robert had forgotten about the dentist. Walking out past his mother he murmurs, "Get rid of the books."

The summer heat is thick outside. Robert wears his toque, the cotton wool, the grey blanket.

It is the same taxi driver. He smiles. During the ride he talks to Robert, his voice sounding like the clatter of teeth pulled one by one and dropped into a hollow bucket. Robert's head is pounding.

At the large building, Robert runs to the doorway, letting his blanket fall on the sidewalk. He is feeling a terrible urgency now, everything is crushing in, everything is roaring down at him, squeezing him into the terrible moment.

He must hang on. Grey fog is everywhere, oozing towards him. He must hang on. Or disappear into the terrible moment, forever.

He runs through the dentist's reception room, fighting to see through the fog, runs past the large-faced woman at the front desk, past the startled patients waiting in a row like ducks at a shooting gallery. His voices are shrieking, hanging from his cotton wool like scabs from a tree. Do this and do this, they say — garbled, confusing commands like radio messages gone wild.

Robert feels he is about to shatter, sees his body exploding into pieces of lifeless machinery, a heap of rusted parts about to be discarded on an endless, empty landscape.

He finds the dentist standing over a patient, drill in hand, his dentist's tunic throbbing vein-blue.

Crying, choking, Robert stands at the doorway. "Pull out my heart!" he screams, then collapses.

The relative who is a social worker is called in to represent the family.

Robert lies before her on the hospital bed, unmoving. The room is bare, a metal screen covers the window. Thirty milligrams of chlorpromazine silence the voices in Robert's veins. Robert does not answer when the relative calls his name.

Outside the day is overcast. Robert does not notice when a seagull lands on his windowsill, squawking. Pays no attention when the relative tells him he can go home providing he makes regular visits to the Mental Health Clinic on Fourth Street. Providing he takes his pills.

Robert at home, sitting on his bed, staring at the dull, grey walls. The room is bare except for his bed and a table. The tinfoil has been removed.

Four times a day his mother gives him a pill and a glass of water. He now shuffles out from his room to take his meals with his parents at the kitchen table, not caring what is placed before him.

Occasionally he will spend an evening in the living room watching television. At these times he will take his father's

THE BIBLE IN LONGHAND

rocking chair and put it directly in front of the television so that his parents must arrange themselves as best they can on either side of him in the darkened room in order to see the screen. In this formation, the three spend the evening staring at the grey flickering light of the television, hour after hour, the staccato sounds of the laugh track the only noise breaking into their silence.

Now that his heart has been removed, now that his body has become a rusted container of grey fog, there is only one voice: Robert understands that this voice belongs to God.

God tells Robert that he must pay for losing his heart, that he must write the Bible out in longhand. Robert informs his mother.

In his room, he sits at his desk. Before him is a stack of loose-leaf paper, a pen and nib, and a bottle of turquoise ink he found in a kitchen drawer.

Outside in the hallway, his parents frantically search the cupboards for the Bible they know they have somewhere.

The relative who is a social worker writes Robert a letter, a pleasant chatty letter, her display of special concern. Robert sends a reply. He addresses the envelope in elaborate Gothic script, using the pen with the nib and the turquoise ink. Inside the envelope he has put three white pages, neatly folded, all blank.

Sixteen months go by as Robert writes out the Bible in longhand. Sixteen hours a day. The slow, elaborate turquoise script. He does not read what he writes, but he is calm.

God does not speak to him until the task has been completed. Then he tells him to write it out again. Once was not enough.

The relative continues to write the occasional letter. When Robert begins to copy the Bible for the second time, he sends the relative a second reply. The same elaborate address, the same three blank pages inside. Except for the third page. In the botton right-hand corner Robert has written, "Godspeed."

Satisfied that Robert has now made significant progress, the relative writes less frequently.

Two years pass. The relative meets Robert's father for coffee.

"He finished the Bible," the father says, "for the second time. And that strange business with the cotton wool. He seems to have settled down."

"That's good," says the relative.

"And he's started going to the Day Programme at Douglas House, that place run by the Mental Health people. Every day a taxi to Douglas House. There are others like him there. Seems to help. And the medicine, when his mother can get him to take it. That helps, too."

"Good," says the relative.

"But he's still the same," the father says. "He'll never change. And his mother worries. What's going to happen to him when we're gone? Who'll look after him then? The plans I had. The travelling I was going to do."

Robert sits at his desk. God has disappeared into the grey fog which now surrounds Robert at all times; he feels safe wrapped in his fog, and sleepy. He can go to sleep whenever he wishes — during the taxi ride to Douglas House, at the supper table, staring at the flat walls of his room — anytime he wants to.

Lately, however, a vertical shaft of light has been appearing before him, more and more frequently. It is like a doorway through the fog, like a sudden break in the clouds that exposes a vast, white plain beyond. This vision doesn't alarm Robert, he feels elation when he sees it.

Sometimes he can make out a group of weeping women hovering about this doorway of light, and to him they are beautiful in their wispy gowns, with their pale, floating hair. He can see, too, that each woman is holding a small, throny tree, and that from the branches of these trees hang tiny, pulsating hearts.

Robert takes up his pen with the nib and writes a third and final letter to his relative:

> Thank you for your kind letters. Aren't the trees wonderful now so many thorny trees and grape hyacinth tulips red roses hanging from their lovely branches everywhere now . . .

The weeping women are calling. Robert, they say, soon you will be with us. Soon you will bring Jack and Barbara to us and their hearts for our lovely trees . . .

CALL OUT OF NOWHERE

We were driving into the city that day, Ellie and Eddy in the front seat, me in the back. I sat still with my hands folded on my lap, dressed up in the green skirt and matching jacket Ellie had made for me as an Easter outfit. I was supposed to be acting excited.

Ellie turned around and grinned. "Smile," she said. "It's wonderful. After all these years, it's wonderful. Isn't it wonderful, Eddy?"

"Wonderful," Eddy said.

I said, "I feel sick. I'm going to throw up."

"Nonsense," Ellie said, "that's just the excitement." She was laughing as if this was the best day of her life.

I sat looking at the back of Eddy's bald head, trying not to think about being sick. Eddy seldom spoke, mostly he nodded. He was nodding now. I watched the mole on the back of his head move up and down, up and down, as he nodded in agreement with what Ellie was saying. Then I looked out the window at all the houses we were passing. When we entered the city, I looked at the buildings, churches, gas stations and parking lots.

When Eddy stopped the car in front of the CPR terminal and said, "We're here," I threw up all over my skirt.

Ellie let out a shriek when she saw the mess. "Now what are we going to do?" she demanded.

Eddy shook his head, his mole moving from side to side. "Clean her up," he said irritably. "What else?"

There weren't any paper towels in the public washroom inside the CPR building so Ellie had to use the stiff, folded sheets of toilet paper which were piled on the lids of the toilets. She made me take off my skirt. Her red lips were a thin slash across her face while she scrubbed at my skirt in the filthy sink.

"Don't just stand there," she hissed. "Start wiping your legs. The train will be here any minute now."

A tall woman came into the washroom, looked at me, smiled and said, "Oh dear!"

She stood beside us at the other sink and combed her hair. Long, yellow hair, patting and shaping it in the mirror before her.

Ellie started talking, the way she always talked to strangers, telling them everything.

"I don't know how I'll ever get her cleaned up in time," she said to the woman. "Her mother's due any minute now. . , hasn't seen the girl in nearly four years . . . and then a call out of nowhere . . . I've been looking after her . . . I'm her aunt . . . Her mother's my brother's wife. It never worked out. I knew from the start it wouldn't. She liked having a good time too much . . . and then my brother had that accident up north so he couldn't look after Judy . . . But my husband said it would break my heart . . . with never knowing when her mother would show up. He said I shouldn't get so involved . . ."

"Come on," I said.

By now I had wiped the vomit from my legs. Ellie gave me back my skirt, blotchy wet in places where she had washed it and still stinking.

The tall woman stared after us with a big, sad look when we left the washroom.

We went into the waiting room. Eddy was leaning against a wall, his arms folded across his chest. He looked mad.

"Cranky," Ellie often said of him. "He's just a cranky old fart."

When we came near him, he grabbed his nose and said, "Pee-U!"

"What time is it?" Ellie said.

"Two-thirty," Eddy said. "Train's late."

I spotted a vending machine at the other end of the room. "I'm thirsty," I said.

Eddy put a hand in his pocket and pulled out the lining. "Empty," he said. He laughed. A joke.

"For heaven's sake," Ellie said, then undid the clasp on her shiny, black purse. She was all dressed up, high heels and her best dress, the purple one with the sequins sewn onto the front, the dress she wore to weddings. She stood a head taller than Eddy. I thought they looked stupid together. She gave me some coins.

I got a cup of Orange Crush from the machine then sat on the green vinyl seat to drink it. I watched Ellie start talking to a man in a brown suit. He looked like he was waiting for someone on the train, too. I knew what she'd be telling him so I stayed where I was.

I thought about my mother. It was hard to remember. Four years ago I was five. I had just learned how to spell ice. I-see-E-for-Ellie. And I'd just gotten my cat, Boots. And my mother had said good-bye again. I was standing in Ellie's kitchen. My mother bent down and hugged me. She was wearing a fur around her neck. Two fox heads sat on either shoulder, their yellow glass eyes staring at the wall behind me.

"Mommy loves you," my mother said. Then she left.

I finished my drink and walked back to where Ellie and Eddy were standing. The man in the brown suit was still beside them.

"And she was always such fun," Ellie was saying, "always such a lot of laughs. Isn't that right, Eddy? Wasn't Judy's mother good at a party? The times we used to have. But hair so thin, she had a terrible time with her hair . . . "

I tugged at Ellie's arm. "I'm hungry," I said.

The man in the brown suit looked away.

Eddy said, "That the whistle? Train must be in."

Right away Ellie started combing my hair. Then people began walking through the door marked ARRIVALS.

Ellie jerked up and down on her toes trying to see above and through all the people. She kept saying, "It won't be long now, Judy, it won't be long."

We waited until the waiting room was empty.

"What did I tell you?" Eddy said.

"I can't understand it," Ellie said. Then she started to cry. "What could have happened? Why didn't she come?"

Eddy said to me, "Come on kid, I'll buy you an ice-cream cone."

"They don't sell ice cream here," I said.

"Then I'll buy you a chocolate bar. Whatever you want. How 'bout a pony?"

We left Ellie sitting on a waiting-room chair, dabbing at her eyes with the sleeve of her dress, and went into the gift shop. I got a Crispy Crunch, a Mars Bar, a six-inch totem-pole candle, a small, white toy seal and a picture postcard of the CPR terminal.

Back in the car, Ellie sniffed and said to Eddy, "How could she do this? She didn't even call."

Eddy didn't nod his head one bit, his mole didn't move an inch.

In the back seat I piled my booty onto my lap. I liked the seal. I didn't know why I had grabbed the totem-pole or the postcard, but I liked the seal. I named it Henry.

I put Henry up to the window as we drove out of the city and whispered to him, "Pretty soon we'll be seeing lots and lots of trees and that will mean we're getting close to Ellie and Eddy's house. Don't you think that will be nice, Henry?"

Henry nodded his furry, white head. I could tell by the way he kept nodding his head that he liked the idea about going home.

ALL THE GOOD AND BEAUTIFUL FORCES

Hey, let me tell you, the trips have been heavy. But like I say to the young ones, the ones with spikes for hair and pins through their noses, enlightenment is a calling, not for everyone. And if they can settle down long enough to hear the truth I tell them this: some people got to be plumbers or brain surgeons and some people got to sell insurance or be gynecologists even, peering up women's snatches all day. But if your own true calling, like mine, is the road to Nirvana, is that drive for Oneness, then you've got to hang in there through the good and the bad. You've got to push through every level of understanding you can and pocket for yourself every bit of universal wisdom like I done. Then you'll be able to dance.

It's probably one of the hardest roads to travel, I tell them, and the way ain't easy, but if you work at it, you can probably get there.

Like for me, the first time nearly blew me away. Seems like a million years ago now. There I was eighteen and still with fuzz on my face and well on my way to oblivion when these two guys from SFU turned me on to some Colombian Gold. Under a bridge on the Fraser River. I was so dumb I thought they were taking me on a canoe trip. Shit, my mother even packed me a lunch. We'd stopped to rest and get out of the rain and just as I was opening up the wax paper around my sandwich, this guy Jim pulls out the Zig Zags and a bag of grass. I hardly knew what the stuff was. Heroin, I thought, alarm bells going. Even expected the cops to swoop down, you know, the usual paranoid view. But that wasn't what did me in. It was later on, after I'd gotten used to the inhaling and holding my breath, when the three of us were standing on the muddy bank grooving on the drizzle and the way the water flowed in time to "Jumpin' Jack Flash" on Jim's transistor radio and this other guy, Brian, I think his name was, said, "Life is terminal, man."

I mean those words hit me like a rocket. I nearly passed out from the truth. I said it out loud, "You live, you die. That's it. There ain't nothing else." I mean I couldn't get over it. My mouth must have hung down to my knees. Brian just nodded his head like he'd let me in on the big joke and I was his latest fool. I guess his trip was ripping the cobwebs from the eyes of snot-nosed innocents like me, but it had an effect. I felt it right down to my core, and all the while I'm trying to get a handle on this heavy revelation my mind's so stretched I was seeing stars throbbing on the leaves of trees, souls fluttering in the breasts of seagulls.

I was so twisted I tried to put my lunch bag over my head, blot it all out, wipe away the awful truth: "You live, you die." I spent weeks after that, going from class to class at the university almost scared to think, but this one idea wouldn't go away and I knew it *never* would. Life was just one big cartoon with Woody Woodpecker at the end of it shrieking like a maniac, "Bid-di-dit, bid-di-dit. That's all folks."

For years that woodpecker kept howling at me and that red head kept turning up, man did it ever! I'd never know what form it would take and then, later on, it settled on my old lady Red but by then it was screaming a different tune: "Do *this* Wilson. Do *that* Wilson," she'd order all the time like some kind of torment.

But, hey, like I said, the path to enlightenment takes work. You don't give up because of irritating shit like woodpeckers or being afraid about living and dying. You got to be on top of all that. Grease the old sy-nap-sees. Get in the groove. That's what I did.

Sure there were bad trips. Ever read Camus on acid?

It was Osley's Blue at somebody's beachhouse. The world went all melted plastic but this chick I was with had Camus in her pack, *The Myth Of Sisyphus*. "Here," she said, "feed on this." After a while I managed to understand what I was reading but that eating idea took hold and pretty soon words started crawling off the page and coming up my arms like worms, like broken spider's legs. And then this one word, "meaninglessness", poked itself right into my eyeballs and into my ears and up my nose so that before long it had gotten into my head, like rot, and taken over. And then everything meant nothing, a big fat zero. So I figured, well if that's the case, there's no way I'm going to push a rock up a hill for the rest of my life, not like my old man, the bathtub salesman. Hell.

So, you see, plenty of good things can come out of a bad trip. It was about that time I dropped out of second year. Hey, if everything was meaningless, I might as well get a lid of dope, ride the Cosmic Elevator, right? Cast my thoughts into the vast useless ether, enjoy the ride. It was the best thing I ever did. I moved in with a bunch of freaks, made candles, sold dope, got by that way.

Yeah, I sure took to dope, must have had the right disposition for it. I mean it was my number one teacher. I learned stuff on dope it would take a dude maybe a thousand years to figure out straight.

Love is part of it too so I've always been into that. Back then, I tell you, it was the Golden Age. Peace. Love. Dove.

Every chick would put out right away, no questions asked, just because you were beautiful. I was calm all the time.

Now and then my old man used to track me down, rattle his tonsils about my hair, about my dropping out of school. My Jesus robe really bugged his ass. I used to say, "Hey man, if you love me it doesn't matter what I look like." "Bullshit," he'd say, "what's love got to do with it? You weren't born to turn into a goddamned vegetable. What are you going to do with the rest of your life?" "Hey, what's the sweat?" I'd say. "When you're dead who gives a fuck?" "Think of your mother," he'd say, by now sounding like a woodpecker, "you're breaking her heart." I'd try to explain, "Hey, man, we're just travelling different roads, that's all. You got a bathtub on your back. Me, I'm carrying the widsom of the universe and anyway what have hearts got to do with it? Trouble with you," I'd tell him, "you don't know what living is. All you care about is selling bathtubs and cutting the lawn and drinking martinis." "That's not true," he'd say, "you just wait till you have children of your own. You just wait till they break your heart." "Shit, man," I'd answer, "nobody owns their kids. What do you think I am, a goddamned goldfish?"

One time he actually smoked some dope with us. In this dump we had on Fourth Avenue. Him in his tie and shirt, his fat belly hanging over his pants, that bathtub on his back, sitting crosslegged around the sand candles with us in the dark. Said he wanted to find out what all this "marijuana business" was about. "Far out!" I said. But stoned, he looked hassled. I could see right into his soul like it was a plate glass window at a department store. Just bathtubs and toaster ovens in there; he was a real disappointment.

And then it turned heavy. It must have been the paregoric we soaked the joints in. Before long everything in the room was on a tilt, like I was standing at the bottom of a mountain and my old man and everybody else was on the top. I felt like

I was being crushed, right in my chest, and I couldn't breathe. And then the mountain turned into a giant bathtub, the whole room was a white enamel bathtub and it started to fill up with water and my father was grinning, he had teeth like chrome bathroom fixtures and I kept yelling, "Pull the plug, we're gonna drown." But everyone else seemed to be swimming just fine, all of them looked like monster goldfish, even my fat old man, he could swim the best. But me, I was drowning. I was gonna die in my father's bathtub and the only thing that could save me was to get out of there and never go near a bathtub or my old man again. And that's what I did.

Anytime I'd happen to see my old man after that I'd get that drowning feeling all over again and have to split, and have to swim for my life.

Fuck, shit, piss, eh? Some trip. Hey, but in living your life there are some things you've got to avoid if you want to stay calm. For a while bathtubs were easy to miss but I had a harder time with woodpeckers. Like for years I was falling in love about once a week. It was all right for the longest time but then one night this big, blonde chick from California, Loralee, showed up with her dog and load of mescaline and it was from Loralee that my path led directly to Red.

Loralee was a turn-on, too bad she didn't stick around. She wore a poncho and cowboy boots and when we got it on her dog would howl like a wolf, the whole world knew what was happening. And Loralee was a real noisy chick, too. Screamed and shouted making love and then wanted more. Nearly did me in. But I could have stayed with her forever. She'd kind of look after me, cook me food, brush my hair. So I followed her to Hornby Island and met some guys she knew there who were into agriculture. There's where I stayed and learned to grow dope.

The country's the place to be, birds and all that natural shit. Stoned, Loralee read my Tarot cards, said I always drew the Death card and that meant I was one heavy dude. Hey, that's me, Wilson, the heavy dude! But I didn't like the idea of carrying Death around on my back. I should have known that the woodpecker was coming close. Just as soon as life and death come into the picture, shaking things up and demanding meaning. I should have known that before long I'd run into Red. It was my Karma.

It happened this one time when I'd been living for ages with the freaks on Hornby Island, minding my own business, growing dope, staying calm. There was this weird guy lived down the road a ways called Ken-Zen and he was into heavy machinery, power wagons, tractors, industrial chain saws. I don't know how it happened but Ken-Zen and I ended up having this contest to see who could chop the most firewood, him with his chain saw or me with an ax. So everybody came. It was a real event, all the freaks and their ladies in long flowered skirts and shawls. This Ken-Zen had said that going back to the land was a pile of shit and he was going to prove that machines were stronger than men. Can't think now why I was picked to take him on but I did and it was a real bummer. He was light years ahead of me with the wood and I nearly broke my goddamned arms trying to keep up with him. After he'd won he strutted off to his cabin laughing like an idiot and I was left in the pile of half-split wood feeling like a useless bastard if ever there was one.

But then there was this chick, someone's friend from the Mainland. I'd never seen her before. Her name, she said, was Red on account of her red hair and the red aura she always had around her. I should have flashed on the woodpecker but I was too freaked out over losing the contest to notice and then Red was being so nice to me. She was real calm, like a soft swollen lake, and she didn't say much that day as we roamed through the woods, except, "I love you, Wilson." She said it a couple of times, "I love you, Wilson." We made love in a clearing covered with moss and wildflowers, shooting stars and some tiny blue flowers were all about, and maybe it was the dope, but that day I guess I loved her too.

Before long she made herself my lady. She always wore this grey blanket made into a long skirt and a black and green lumber jacket. She drank Calona Red for breakfast. Next thing I knew, I'd knocked her up.

Red knew of this place called Sombrio Beach, just up the coast from Sooke, where there were some empty shacks on the beach. It was getting to be spring so we went there. We found a cabin that was pretty rotten in this cove but figured we could fix it up with driftwood and some plastic. Everyone else was doing that down there. We were getting welfare so the money was no sweat. It was a gas to hitch a ride into Sooke for supplies and get pots and pans from the Sally Ann and sacks of brown rice and pinto beans from the health food store and bring the stuff back to our shack on the beach. It was neat in there, like a fort I'd had as a kid. We made a bed out of cedar boughs and an old sleeping bag and I fixed up some shelves using flat pieces of driftwood I found on the beach.

It was incredible, too, having all that welfare bread. The dope we could buy! And we lived pretty good, got rock cod off the beach and mussels and clams off the rocks. Now and then straight campers would hike down the cliff to the beach for the day and then find they couldn't carry all their stuff back with them. It was like Christmas then, we'd be given hot dogs and buns, jugs of wine, Oreo cookies, bags of potato chips. One time we were left three sirloin steaks. Shit, did we have a feast that night! During that time on the beach we did a fair bit of acid and when it came summer and got hot we went naked all day. Boy, did that blow the campers' minds!

Yeah, we were a real community of freaks down there, living calm and easy. But then it got heavy.

Winter came and the rain. That place was like living inside a plastic bag. Everything was wet all the time and then Red started bitching like a regular fishwife. I'd seen it coming all summer: she'd get her bird claws into me over every little thing. Like where was I going whenever I'd wander down the beach with Anabel, two shacks down, or why didn't I come straight home after a trip to Sooke, how come I had to stay away for a week? She started acting like she owned me. You'd think I wore a three-piece suit all day or something and then that shitless winter she started screaming, "Why don't you get a job, Wilson? Why don't we get a proper house, Wilson?" I sure found out what that red aura of hers meant. Trouble, man.

Here she was turning into that woodpecker, that "you live, you die" woodpecker and making all the stuff in between a colossal bad trip. And there I was in her cage somehow, in the goddamned bird cage with her, and I couldn't get out because I was tied. She had that kid in her stomach and it was mine. I was tied because I thought then I wanted that kid.

I did acid the night Red finally had it. I felt like I was on the moon. Just whirling around in space. There was this storm crashing branches outside the cabin and I thought it was meteors and stars we were banging into. It was cold in there, too. The beach wood was so wet it only fizzled when I lit it.

This guy from the next cabin came in and did some chants with an eagle feather over Red . He was a skinny guy with red acne crud all over his face but he sure had soul, the way he said those chants, all about spirits and stars and the universe. It was heavy duty, made me think of God. And just one candle burning, too, made me think of nativity scenes on Christmas cards. It was about that time of the year, and for a moment I felt swollen up with warmth like I was Joseph and Red was Mary and maybe this kid inside her was another Jesus about to be born, my Jesus, my boy. I rode on that thought for most of the night until Red, with her usual woodpecker screech, started complaining about her pains and shrieking so much I had to go outside and sit under a tree. That frosted me off. In all that rain. And then that drowning business started all over again. I was sitting in a bathtub and all the rain was going to fill it up and I was going to drown. The guy with the eagle feather came outside just as I was yelling, "Get out, get out, the ship's sinking," and he grabbed me and pulled me from the water. "It's a girl," he said, "Vishnu Meadowlark."

Not long after that I split. I don't know what I expected of that kid, maybe to come varooming out on a bike or something, but I sure wasn't into all that crying and stink. Red carried on with her woodpecker ways, killing any good feeling I'd ever had about the kid, or her, even. She wanted me to do all the work, too, like hike up the cliff about fifteen times a day to get a ride to Sooke for supplies. And it was winter, too. "Get some food, Wilson." "Gather some wood, Wilson." "Here, Wilson, look after the baby." Shit, man, I ain't nobody's slave. And Red got so fat after the kid, she ballooned up like a giant spider, and all the time shouting orders at me, breaking my balls. I had to get out of there.

Lucky for me my grandmother croaked about then and left me some dough. I got the hell away from Red and that kid and did it ever feel good to split out of that cage, like I'd busted out of jail. No more of Red's screaming, no more hauling wood, freezing my ass in that shack. I headed for Vancouver.

Before I knew it Anabel from the beach had found me. That's chicks for you. Soon as they sniff any free bread they're on you like a dirty blanket. Anabel kept feeding me a line about how much she loved me and what a heavy dude I was.

Hey, I wasn't immune! I let her be my lady for a while but deep down I figured, no way was a chick going to get the best of me again.

Anyways, after going to Europe on my grandmother's money and then living in Mexico for a while, and then in an Oregon commune, I finally ended up on Salt Spring Island, where I've been ever since. Living by myself, staying clear of people trying to change me.

But, hey, the trips I've had. Nothing too heavy, though just small, beautiful adventures, and no more of that woodpecker stuff either, none of that.

But I don't know where the time's gone, months just fly by like fence posts on a highway, whole years are a distant, golden blur. It's like a speeded-up movie, but a good movie, one that's beautiful. And anyways, time's not where it's at. These days I'm into dancing, any kind of dancing. I'm into joy and celebration; I'm going to dance till I ain't no more. There's so much to feel good about, so many reasons to dance. I got these two cats, Sam and Annie, they're like people, follow me all round my place. We communicate, we understand each other. And my garden. I grow tomatoes, kohlrabi, potatoes and kale, all organic, none of that chemical crap in my food.

But people when they see me now at the Saturday morning market, they think I'm just another old hippie selling candles. It slays me. They think I'm brain-damaged, living in some time warp from the sixties. Shit with sauce, they look at my bald head, at my beard, and they think I'm some kind of basket case.

But, hey, they don't know what these eyes are seeing, they can't ever understand what I know. I'll bet none of them can get up and dance whenever the spirit moves them. I'm open to forces they'll never even dream about.

Like last week in the drug store. I get this rush, a golden glow all through my nerve endings and I hadn't even smoked dope or done anything. Just straight and crazy. But warm, man, but hot to dance. So I grab this old broad who's stocking the shelves and try to twirl her down the aisle to the Muzak but shit if she doesn't scream, her old face just cracked like concrete. "Help, help!" she yells. "Feel the spirit," I say, "get in the Cosmic Groove, lady, we're all children of the Universe," but she grabs this bottle of Pepto Bismol and cracks it across my head. Pretty soon there's the pharmacist pulling at my poncho and next thing I know I'm in the back of a cop car. "Take it easy, Wilson," the cop says. "Settle down, Wilson."

But that's the trouble with people, they're always freaking out over small shit like that. They got souls the size of shrivelled peas. That old broad said I smelled. But it was her that stank, must have had about gallon of perfume on her, strong enough to make you gag. Put a match to her and she'd explode. Me, I smell natural, like earth, like dirt. Keep the oils on the body where they belong.

But they don't see any of that. They keep hassling me about my dancing. And I'm not even on the dole any more! Shit, I sell enough dope, I make enough candles to get by pretty well without it. But the cops are always on my case anyway. They want to squash my dancing, they want to stop me from doing it in public. "No way," I tell them, "I dance to the rhythm of the Universe." But they just laugh when I say that, like I was a retard or something.

Most nights I get ripped and go out to the field back of my rented place. Nobody bothers me there. Sam and Annie always follow and watch from a rotten log by the side of the field. I go out to dance under the stars or in the rain and fog, it doesn't matter, but I always dance alone. I start by standing perfectly still and letting the forces of the universe enter into me, like strong warm rays, all the good and beautiful forces. I give myself up to them and then when I open my eyes I see clear blue crystal everywhere like an ice palace and the shadows are smiling. And then I dance. I'm in touch then and I dance. It's a swirling, whirling dance like planets in motion, like heavenly bodies careening through space. And then I know that time doesn't exist anymore. I'm in the continuous present and death's defeated, death's not even in the picture.

Sometimes I dance all night. I lose my body and I'm just this red and living spirit floating around my field. And sometimes Sam and Annie seem to be dancing too. I see their flashing cat's eyes moving through the inky blackness and I know they're with me, that they're in touch.

When I dance in my field, everything's gone, all the bad shit, the cops, the chicks with their woodpecker claws, people trying to change you, make you small. And I'm free and large and nothing matters. My soul is a net as huge as the world and I dance it outward in larger and larger circles until I have completely covered the Universe and I am one with it. And then I'm close, man, I'm near Nirvana.

MACARONI AND CHEESE

From: *The We-Used-To-Be-The-Middle-Class Cookbook*

The first time I served my family Macaroni and Cheese you might find this amusing my youngest son said What's this Mom? and pushed it away never having seen macaroni before let alone tasting it and not knowing that this was what poor people ate and now that his parents were no longer middle-class there would be a lot more Macaroni and Cheese dinners in his five-year-old future.

The first time I served it I cried yes I did. I served it on a Tuesday when there were no more leftovers not wanting to give up roast beef on Sundays some things are sacred. I served it carried it on a silver service tea-tray a wedding gift from Bud's great-aunt the one with the money left to cancer research and we ate it at the dining-room table not the kitchen table sometimes you have to be brave.

I served a nice little salad with it too and even put the ketchup in a small cut-glass bowl because ketchup bottles on the table are dreadful. The milk too went into a pretty glass pitcher not the milk carton on the table no never the carton. But finally it was Macaroni and Cheese for dinner and I cried not boo hoo but hot squinty tears when Bud said pass the salad and pouted yes he did I could tell that hurt pouty look of his he was thinking not even a strip of bacon for godsake.

The trouble was I had never made Macaroni and Cheese before and who would I mean ever want to? I had tried a complicated recipe since I pride myself on my ability to read books do sums choose colours but what I didn't know was that this Macaroni and Cheese called for oh my god a milk sauce. And the other thing I didn't know was that with a milk sauce the milk has to be added slowly mother's told me since. How was I to know? The sauce was lumpy oh no lumpy sauce so that bits of uncooked white yes cancer-causing bleached white flour would come away in our mouths. My mouth, Bud's hurt pouty mouth, Jason Jeremy Jasper's round pink trusting mouths sucking on lumpy Macaroni and Cheese. Like sawdust said Bud it's good said Jason Jeremy. Goo said Jasper.

But Bud but Bud all Bud could do was pout sniff pout sniff then snort This looks like barf he said yes he did like barf. It's true I wailed like barf Cathy Grant serves her family barf from a silver service tea-tray cut-glass bowl pretty pitcher at the dining room table and oh what's to become of us?

I'm sorry so sorry I said Macaroni and Cheese is not ever is never ever the thing to feed an upwardly mobile white Caucasian male used to Coq au Vin Waldorf Salad Chocolate Mousse lying about all day now reading spy novels not looking for Engineer work any work. Don't be mad I should never have done it slap my hand Cathy Cathy naughty Cathy make something interesting with crackers vacuum bags kitty litter god knows I've tried hard to economize. Every magazine knows this for the truth I have them all *Chatelaine Women's Own Family Circle Western Living Ladies Digest* tasty tempting morsels for pennies for nothing. Yes there's Africa I should be thankful but the magazines don't help too many olives pimentos kiwi fruit mushroom soup mini-mallows cost too much.

MACARONI AND CHEESE

Nevertheless if only there was a cookbook for people like us for the newly poor rambling around in our good lives with not a cent to spend at dollar-forty-nine day not even one piece of lint. If only there was a cookbook to help those of us who used to be middle-class and who are now god help us out of work the nouveau poor and having to this whole lesser life *adjust*.

To the whole idea of budget. Can't can't can't spend like we used to. Teach old dogs new tricks like making budget a state of mind now that shopping as a way of life has cruelly ended oh it's going going gone.

Surely there must be a book about it something for smart up-to-date women like me yes I am in no need to be falsely modest. I read books do sums choose colours. Well well well. How to make hamburger casseroles for instance that don't taste like sawdust goo milk sauce don't taste like brown rice dry Third World bland. Yes I'm thankful. But show me point the way to cook healthy cook cheap cook *very* interestingly amusingly on pennies next to nothing. Make my husband smile oh make Bud smile.

I grieve yes I do for some handy little book which could point the way without getting weird getting religious. Something I could put with pride on my kitchen counter something fun. Nice pictures. Could pass around show Joan show Vicky Gail Jane Pauline the latest thing. Mother too Aunt Bee.

Some way there's got to be some way I can go on looking like Cathy Grant that Bud can go on looking like Bud Grant on the outside. Some way I can fill us up with Regular instead of Super as it were till Bud gets work does something.

Clunk. Clunk. What if he doesn't. What if finally after all it comes down to desperate Macaroni and Cheese on the best china probably sold. What if what if that's all that happens before I die some horrible lumpy milk sauce death with bits of unmelted cheese what everyone knows poor people eat. Of my own making. You make your own Macaroni and Cheese you lie in it. But never Kraft Dinner. No never some things are principles are sacred. Never ever serve that I'd sooner die not even as a joke. Oh what's to become of us?

I could heaven forbid get a job work get liberated drive a tractor sell jewelry sell clothes minimum wage. Jason Jeremy Jasper's mother a working person poor. Read books do sums choose colours for a fee by the hour? Bud forever reading Helen MacInnes John Le Carré. Furious face to the end to find out who did it.

To me? What if we start eating in our undershirts picking our teeth with matchbook covers wearing old grey wool gloves without fingers? Pick over bargain basement bins looking for something cheery yellow polyester? God forbid polyester. And Jason Jeremy Jasper turning dirty out of control eventually into mean adolescents causing social workers school counsellors juvenile judges to impose on us. Impose. Down to one car sell the house pitch a tent. No rent a welfare basement one-bedroom suite raining all the time spots on the rug.

Become less than middle-class less than average. All this life wading that wide wonderful road in middle centre between heady glitter and dirt on your face disgrace. All this life pushed off the shoulder nevertheless falling having been pushed by statistical restraint. Falling like Alice and no How-To Books in sight no good solid formulas pointing the way how to be un-middle-class. How to adjust with style same on the outside no one need know how to have Bud smile again oh have Bud smile. What's to become of us? Nothing other than this whine my god we've run out of pennies run out. Of ideas there's no other way to be just the middle way no other worthwhile proper way to be no way up except lottery every way down. And terrible out. We're out. Fallen angel oh my god I'm going to start crying start crying really cry and never stop amusing no?

CLUB SANDWICH

It's balloons. I've got to have twelve brightly-coloured helium-filled balloons. One for each sub-section of the Charter. Where am I going to get twelve such balloons at this time of night? All the clowns are in bed. I should have forseen this. Now it may be too late. All this striving hard work yearning come to naught. Holy harlequin. Woe is me!

I know, I'll get Ernie. Ernie wake up!

My husband Ernie. White overweight middle-income wage-earner likes to fish. Wake up darling. Reel me in a balloon.

No, no Ernie. Do me a clown.

What, says Ernie, what right now? But it's three a.m. in the morning, I say it's three a.m. You want a clown?

Yes, yes my darling bundle of fat cells. A clown.

How does it go? says Ernie. Top or bottom? Funny or slapstick? Tell me Margaret. How does it go?

Three-thirty a.m. Ernie in clown suit. White face red ball nose yellow mop wig polka dot suit duck feet. Turn around Ernie, let me see you.

Do you realize, says Ernie, that I've got a basement to plaster at 8:30 this morning I say 8:30?

CLUB SANDWICH

Oh it's not right, I wail, there's no balloons! I need twelve brightly-colored helium-filled balloons. With ribbons. To go with you.

What for? yawns Ernie.

The Charter, I sniff moan whimper.

Oh that. Can't you fake it, says Ernie, I'm tired.

Poor round baby. Let him for the moment sleep. Yes, I'll have to fake it.

I'll just throw on this raincoat over my nightie, slip on rubberboots and then be off.

To Hop Sing's, all-night seller of ordinary balloons. I'll have three packs please. Dismal-looking things though. Half an inch wide. Three inches long. And all mostly yellow like lifesavers, hardly any red or green. Still I'm desperate. I'll do anything. Got to be ready by six only two hours to go. Or this forty-eight hours will be for naught.

Back home. Now to find the air pump.

Ernie, wake up I call. My Ernie-clown asleep. Ernie!

Here, he flaps into the room duck feet first, have a sandwich. I'll just go find the air pump.

Oh my darling Ernie. My saviour. My round pudgy jewel. His wide red clown lips smiling. My Ernie-toons.

I bite into my sandwich, what looks like lettuce and tomato on brown. Ernie, I call, this lettuce is tough.

Quack, says Ernie from the basement. Quack. Quack. Quack.

I pull the lettuce from the sandwich. Inspection time. Oh Ernie not this not your green boxer shorts. Pretend lettuce.

Bite my ass growl-grins Ernie, here's the air pump.

We work furiously. Pop. Pop. Balloons are popping.

Slow down, says Ernie shaking his yellow mop hair, the things I do for you.

Knee to knee, clown suit to rain coat, yellow mop head to grey Afro over the air pump on the bedroom floor. Ernie and I.

Is it worth it? asks Ernie, surrounded by balloons mostly yellow one blue.

Not funny, I say. You have Elks have fishing now the kids have gone what have I got?

Me, says my Ernie my darling true one. Me!

Oh no, I broke the only red balloon. I broke it. I need one red balloon for sub-section 3, the clause about vibrancy, life. Outgoing red. Red for daring do. Cornerstone of the code.

We'll spray-paint a yellow one says Ernie my hope.

There now. Twelve balloons. One clown.

But the ribbons. There's got to be ribbons! Half an hour to go. I'll just slip these white satin ones from the children's christening gowns, staple them together to get the proper length hope it passes muster.

There.

My wonderful clown my Ernie standing outside Ramona Stephens' three-bedroom split-level six a.m. this Friday morning. Dew still on the grass a dog barking somewhere. Ramona Stephens Grand Master. The last hurdle.

On her front lawn me in my nightie raincoat rubberboots. I give Ernie a final check. Re-do his lips redden them. Tostle his yellow mop hair. But will the balloons do I moan into this white face red nose. Twelve long balloons filled with ordinary air. Will they do? They flop they droop. They look like twelve exclamation marks gone sad.

I've done everything the application form required, taken my mother out to lunch at a family restaurant and had the waitresses bring a cake with sparklers and sing Happy Birthday (mother enjoyed it even if it wasn't her birthday); drank five vodka and tonics at the Ladies' Bridge then tap-danced to Yankee Doodle Dandy after the tea and finger sandwiches, took an old-age pensioner (Mrs. Wilkinson) to a Ladies Only Strip Show, she was amazed "they" came in such a variety of sizes, dressed as Klondike Kate and stood on a busy street corner for two hours collecting for the disease of my choice (Alcoholism).

All within forty-eight hours. These are the rules. You get one chance one chance only to be admitted to the Club. It's all or nothing.

Ernie rings Ramona Stephens' doorbell. I crouch behind a rhododendron. The painted red balloon is dripping over the front steps. Drip. Drip.

Ramona Stephens opens the door peers uncertainly outside. Pink foam curlers (I didn't know!). Blue dressing gown. She sees Ernie. She smiles. Is she smiling?

This is it.

My rotund Ernie hands Ramona Stephens the balloons. He sings my greeting to the tune of Hello Dolly. Louder Ernie. I can barely hear you.

> *Well hello Ramona, you're looking swell Ramona*
> *It's so good to see you smile on this fine morn*
> *I sure can tell Ramona, it's over hell Ramona*
> *That you're middle-aged, your passion's frayed*
> *But you're still one real fun gal.*

With feeling, Ernie. Give it all you've got.

Oh never dull Ramona, full of life Ramona
That's our Credo, you sure know how to throw a pie
So . . . . consider Margaret, Ramona
She's a million laughs Ramona
She'll be a credit
She'll be a real fun gaalllllll.

Done, it's over. Ramona Stephens shuts the door. Ernie gets up off his knees. Here comes the paper-boy.

Ernie my corpulent cupcake you were swell.

Nuts, says Ernie, I'm hungry.

At breakfast. Ernie eating. Back to workman. It's 7:30 Margaret I say 7:30 in the morning and I've not had one moment's sleep.

Phone rings. It's Ramona Stephens. Yes. Yes. Oh . . . .

Oh no! I've been rejected Ernie. My application's been rejected. For lack of spunk. Alcoholism doesn't count. My balloons lacked get-up-and-go. You're a wage-earner Ernie. Oh I've been rejected by the Club. Woe is me.

Look at it this way, says Ernie my dream, they're not the only game in town.

Wheels turning. So true my bald love my heart. So true.

It's green boxer shorts I say. Ernie I've got to have those green boxer shorts. I'll send Ramona Stephens a Club Sandwich. Lettuce and Tomato on brown. Pretend lettuce.

Quack quack says Ernie my round one my life. I'll deliver. But first, he says, I'll just use those shorts. We've run out of I say run out of toilet paper haven't we?

FRENCH FRIES

June evening fast driving the highway into town past the men's slo-pitch game back of the community hall. And the fans the families gathered on the green bleachers or standing at the edge of the diamond behind a ten-foot protective fence hands in pockets last inning in the fast-fading light. And the kids scattered along the side road young boys in soccer jackets climbing a mound of dirt out front the turquoise-and-yellow portable toilets or running after wild balls dangerously close to the traffic.

I pull into Hannigan's Take-Out nearby a brown box on a double lot beside Safeway thinking I've time to kill before home and let him put the kids to bed for once I don't get out that much yet isn't it somehow bold to go to a place by yourself to eat somehow it's like reckless adventure. But that's the way it's lately gone I'm always in the middle of a group of kids five four and two not that I mind but still there's only them to watch. I'm always saying be careful like it was a prayer or a protective net I throw as they head into vacant pools stairs without carpet unknown driveways gravelled to cut their tender knees. *Be careful* I call at least I would have said it should they be served up dead having fallen drowned or slipped away from my gaze should I have watched something else say a distant attractive man or an interesting couple just for a second taken my eyes off them only for a second.

Not me I always watch them.

But now I am let loose never having thought it could be so good lucky for me my aunt is sick and needing attention that I could take the night alone to visit and have this slow time going home. Men never know the sweet cage we mothers are imprisoned in.

But here I am at Hannigan's Take-Out. It's looking like a perfect church and I enter it solemlnly giving thanks and I welcome the pungent smell and the moist close air and I shuffle into the tiny space in the line-up to take my place.

A mother on the loose and with wonderful decision I say after the fat woman in shorts ahead orders soft ice cream I say *An order of fries*. All for me no sharing no handing out my fries to those other ones those little ones who require their separate plates and things to be exactly equal. All for me alone *An order of fries* I declare like singing then take my place against the wall.

Two giant boys come next no more than twelve but bigger than adults they've legs so thin like two by fours it's hard to see your own small boy so large so strangely grown remote. They're shy they whisper onion rings then take fantastic legs to stand inside the corner by the door and oh the giant feet that wait.

I watch the walls they're white but seem to drip I notice smears of ketchup thick and brown behind my head and sticky splashes of Coke or root beer on the floor. The woman behind the counter my mother's age grey hair and glasses yellow smock cannot be heard to speak but passes slips of paper silently to the youth behind the grill. We customers wait in silence thick we wait.

A man comes in he has a child a boy who's seven maybe eight they gaze at the menu white on red above the grill then order faintly but I hear two hot dogs no relish two Cokes with ice.

FRENCH FRIES

And all is quiet no one speaks there's just the sizzle of the grill the ice that clunks in paper cups the woman slowly buttering buns.

I read the bulletin board lose myself in the bulletin board it seems I'm gone for days. The squares of paper with the even-cut fringe they tell of trucks like new and houses of furniture that must be sold and Deep Cove man with truck will haul and babysitting by the hour or day. There's perms and a notice for Casino Night on the 24th from 9 to 1 and a Beer Garden at the Sanscha Hall on Canada Day the Dogwood Band will play.

Maybe we should go get out for a while I think just him and me why not go out in the day for a change the two of us drive off in the car like a date leave the kids behind at the open front door and Grandma will come from her apartment to mind. Imagine whole conversations without a break and nobody on my lap to sit at those wooden tables at the Sanscha Hall and drink Labatt's for a dollar-twenty-five and look around all over the place and dizzy myself with seeing.

I turn from the board fulfilled my reckless eyes they stop for a moment at the eight-year-old boy he has what appears to be a nail file treacherous thing he's picking at his thumb his father doesn't seem to care but soon I know there'll be blood on his shirt and worry for an instant a mother again but then behold he is not mine and my eyes sweep wonderfully on.

Outside to the gentle pink I look through the window through the smudged glass door to the soundless lot and the teenaged boys parked side by side. The traffic noiseless moves on by.

I'm peaceful like that hour at night when the kids have finally gone to sleep when dreamily I can let my mind go limp at last let it finally wander. Then release my eyes from their domestic ties and look at a book or look outside if it's summer at the street or wander in the vegetable patch or stop at the bachelor's button planted four years back and marvel how they re-seed themselves how year after year they grow.

This Hannigan's Take-Out sanctuary more solemn than a church.

And then the bell to call me back my fries are done the bell like a small metal breast upon the counter top it clangs my fries are done. The onion rings too the woman has for the boys just as a crowd of baseball players shove through the door and some remove their caps.

I let the boys take their order first and then I take my fries.

Long golden fingers sparkling in their fat like the ads all say they lie in a cardboard dish they yearn for salt and pepper malt vinegar too from a tall glass jar. I get a small quick smile from the woman as I ask for extra salt then change my mind and order a Coke to go to take through the men the baseball players towards the door. This is the hardest part a young woman on the loose and baseball players arranged like bowling pins before the door.

Blue uniforms with a red-and-white stripe down the leg and on their chests says *Men-o-paws* because I guess they're over forty and unafraid to glare and do. Good-naturedly and at each other then a path is made like an honour guard or a dangerous sea which is suddenly parted and as I move through one turns around has TERRY on his back and 43.

He winks and lets me out the door I smile my thanks then reach the car prepare to close up shop. Time it's time to put my eyes back in their case take them back to where they're firmly held.

It's getting dark it's getting late those little ones will be in bed and calling for their mother's kiss it's only a five-minute

FRENCH FRIES

drive to home. And he'll be wondering where I am in front of the TV set with his bedtime snack he'll be worrying why I've been away so long. I prepare to head for home can't wait now to head for home.